Red Jade

Also by the author

Chinatown Beat
Year of the Dog

Red Jade

Henry Chang

Published by
Soho Press, Inc.
853 Broadway
New York, NY 10003

Library of Congress Cataloging-in-Publication Data
Chang, Henry, 1951–
Red jade / Henry Chang.
p. cm.
ISBN 978-1-56947-859-2
1. Yu, Jack (Fictitious character)—Fiction. 2. Chinese—United
States—Fiction 3. Organized crime—Fiction.
4. Chinatown (New York, N.Y.)—Fiction. I. Title.
PS3603.H35728R43 2010
813'.54—dc22
2010027922

10 9 8 7 6 5 4 3 2 1

For Andrew,

My brother, the first born, who covered the straight and narrow so that I could run, wild and free, down these Chinatown streets, slipping off the yoke of what we were *expected* to be in Chinese America.

You proved that all things are possible through dedication and determination and a dash of Destiny. Thanks for the Beavers, the Tracers, the "Chinatown Angels," and *Paradise* in Harlem, but most of all, for sharing this blood.

Peace and love, always.

Acknowledgments

Many thanks go to Geoff Lee, Jan Lee, and Eddie Cheung at Sinotique, Doris Chong for the inspiration, Alvin Eng for the good Words, The Emperor's Club for spreading the love through music, Benilda Ayon, Liz Martinez, Debbie Chen in Houston, and my NYC *hindaai* posse for keeping me grounded.

Special thanks to my editor Laura Hruska, Ailen Lujo and the Soho Press crew, and to Dana and Debbie for crunching the numbers and cheering me on.

For Seattle, I'm grateful to Doug Moy, Chandra and Jason, Linsi and Brandon for the great hospitality, and to Maxine Chan for the keen insight.

I'm indebted to M.C., attorneys Joann Quinones and Keith Smith for the legal aid.

A shout-out goes to Chef George Chew the man, and to Marilynn K. Yee, photog *extraordinaire*.

And at last, much love and thanks to Maria Chang, for the long leap of faith.

Red Jade

Dark Before Dawn

"Rise up! Yu! Yuh got bodies!"

It was the overnight sarge calling from the 0-Nine, the Ninth Precinct, growling something about Manhattan South detectives into his ear, barking out a location with two bodies attached to it.

As soon as Jack Yu caught the address, he knew: *Chinatown again.* He was going back to the place he'd left behind when he moved to Brooklyn's Sunset Park, just across the river but a world away.

It always started with the rude awakening, the alarms going off in his head, the angry clamor, and then the Chinatown darkness snatching him off again, back into the Fifth Precinct, back to unfinished business. . . .

He'd been dead asleep, dreaming he was still partying at the After–Chinese New Year's party that Billy Bow had pulled together at Grampa's, aka the Golden Star Bar and Grill, a favorite Chinatown haunt. In this dream, Jack was picturing himself feeding quarters into the big jukebox setup, a rock tune with a deep bass pounding out, *Hey son where ya going with dat gun in ya hand?* He's gulping back a beer, scoping out the revelers. *Gonna shoot ma lady, she cheat'in wit annuda man.*

Jack spots Alexandra. *Alex.* Friend and confidante, wearing a bright red Chinese jacket, the color of luck, glowing in the darkness of the bar. She nods at him and jiggles her smile to the backbeat, her long black hair shimmering in the dim blue light. *Gonna shoot her down, down to the ground,* wailing from the jukebox. He wants to pull Alex close, to bring her heart to heart, to kiss her eyes lightly and find out what she's thinking. But suddenly there's this clamor, from the back of his head, accelerating to his frontal lobe, like a thundering lion drum starting up, following the raucous clash of brass cymbals and iron gongs, exploding suddenly into jarring, blinding consciousness.

He reached toward the frantic pleas of the noise, the cell phone's cry, the alarm clock's clang. The clock radio banged out a steady beat. Jack looped the beaded chain over his head; the gold detective's badge tumbled, then its weight held the chain taut. He'd moved to Brooklyn and changed precincts after Pa's death, but still he hadn't escaped the old neighborhood. He rolled his neck, popped the ligaments, pulled on his clothes.

He patted down his thermal jacket for the plastic disposable camera, and dropped his Colt Detective Special into a pocket.

He took the stairs down and stepped into the freezing wind, letting the cold rain pelt his face, pumping up his adrenaline. He jogged down to Eighth Avenue in the desolate darkness, and jumped into one of the Chinese *see gay,* car service lined up along the street of all-night fast-food soup shacks. He badged the driver, giving the address in Cantonese while slipping him a folded ten-spot.

"Go," Jack said, "*Faai di,* quick. I'm in a hurry."

The driver made all the green lights and the short-cut

turns. He blazed the black car across the empty Brooklyn Bridge and dropped Jack off at Doyers Street, off the Bowery in the original heart of Chinatown.

The trip had taken twelve screeching minutes.

Seven Doyers was a four-story walk-up right on the bend of the old Bloody Angle, where the tong hatchetmen of the past battled and bled over turf and women, butcher-sharp cleavers hidden under their quilted Chinese jackets.

Jack knew the street well; it was around the corner from where he'd grown up, where his pa had passed away recently. And around the corner from where his former blood brother Tat "Lucky" Louie had met his fate: shot in the head, he was now comatose at Downtown Hospital.

The Bloody Angle was a serpentine, twisting street that was anchored on the Bowery end by a Chinese deli, two small restaurants, and a post office branch. Where the street cut to the right and dipped down, there was a stretch of Chinese barbershops and beauty salons on both sides.

Doyers was a Ghost street and everyone knew it. The Ghost Legion was the dominant local gang that terrorized Chinatown, and Lucky had been their *dailo,* their leader. Normally, Lucky would have been Jack's source for information about gangland politics, but his condition had ended such cooperation.

Seven Doyers stood above a Vietnamese restaurant and the Nom Hoy Tea Parlor on an empty street lined with the closed, roll-down gates used overnight. The uniformed officer standing outside was a solitary figure beneath the yellow glow of the old pagoda-style streetlamp; a tall, baby-faced Irish kid, a rookie. Jack wondered how he'd pulled the overnight shift. Had he been desperate for overtime or had he fucked up somehow; was this a reward or punishment?

Jack, letting his gold badge dangle, asked, "So who called it in?"

"Dunno," the rookie answered with a shrug, "Sarge just told me to stay here and secure the scene. Wait for *you*. Yu?" The kid grinned.

"Where's the sarge at?" Jack asked, looking at the entrance.

"Dunno," the rookie repeated. "He got a call from the captain and he left."

Jack didn't see a squad car anywhere. His watch read 5:45 AM. "Who was here when you arrived?"

"An old *Chinaman*," he answered, pausing, allowing for a reaction from Jack, who didn't rise to the bait. Jack offered instead the *inscrutable* yellow face.

"He said he was the father," the rookie continued. "And that there were two dead bodies inside."

"So where's he now?"

"Dunno. He left after the sarge left."

"Did he say anything?"

"Who?"

"The old *Chinese-American*," Jack said.

"Oh. Said he had to make a phone call. Or something. Hard to understand his funky English."

Jack shook his head disdainfully, scanning the empty street. "Keep an eye out," he advised.

"Ten-four," the rookie responded, straightening up as Jack entered the building.

Death Before Dishonor

The door at the top of the first flight of rickety stairs was slightly ajar. Yellow Crime Scene tape crossed its frame.

Jack pulled the tape back and took a breath. He pushed the door gently, stepping into the space illuminated by dim fluorescent light. The old apartment was a typical Chinatown walk-up: a big rectangular room, sparsely furnished, with a kitchenette and a small bathroom against a long wall. Worn linoleum covered the floor. The rest of the space was open. A little table nestled in the corner to his left, a puffy jacket draped over a chair.

The place looked neat; there were no signs of a struggle.

Even in the half-light, Jack saw them right away: two bodies, holding hands but sprawled apart, on their backs, across the width of a bed in the far corner. Their legs dangled off the side of the bed. One man, one woman, Chinese, as far as he could make out in the shadowy distance.

The woman still had her quilted coat on.

There was a lady's handbag placed neatly against the foot of the bed.

On the linoleum at the headboard end was a small clock radio, crash-tilted at an angle to the floor, its digital display frozen at 4:44 AM.

As he stepped closer, he figured the dead couple to be in

their mid-thirties. He couldn't find a pulse, but the bodies were still warm to the touch. Rigor had not set in.

Dead less than two hours, Jack thought.

He pulled the plastic disposable camera from his jacket.

The man still had two fingers of his right hand on the butt of a gun, a small black revolver, just at the end of his grasp, dangling askew off the duvet cover. He was grimacing; dark blood spread from the back of his head. In the firm grip of his left fist was the woman's right hand, their fingers laced, as if he was taking her with him somewhere. There was blood on the back of her right hand, blood on the comforter that had come from inside her palm, and a small red hole in the center of her forehead. Beneath that, a dark puddle had formed in the turned-up collar of her coat. Her eyes were open, and her lips slightly parted; she wore a look of disbelief.

In the space between the two bodies was a crumpled business card. Protruding from the man's shirt pocket was a folded piece of notepaper.

Jack stepped back and snapped photographs from different angles and distances, wide shots and close-ups fixing the images in his mind before Crime Scene arrived.

At 4:44 AM, the woman wasn't going out, Jack thought. She'd just come home. And he was waiting for her, his jacket draped over the chair. No sign of forced entry. He'd had a key. Or she'd let him in.

The layout of the bodies made it look like she'd sat down at the edge of the bed, placed her handbag on the floor, and then he'd shot her. She'd fallen straight back, nestled neatly into the comforter. Dead on impact, a bullet in her brain, the back of her head bleeding out, he concluded.

Sometime after, the man had seated himself, taken her hand in his, and then eaten the gun.

Jack imagined it with a cold clarity—the gun jerking out of the man's mouth, the wild swing of his arm smashing into the clock radio, sending it to the floor. The revolver bouncing, sliding onto the comforter.

The crashed clock radio on the floor was blinking 4:44 AM, offering the three worst numbers a Chinese could get: the number four in Cantonese sounded like death. *Triple* death.

The man had drop-twisted to his right, as if he were dragging her into the next life—holding hands—toward oneness with the universe.

The gun was an older model H&R 622, a .22-caliber revolver that fit the Saturday Night Special profile. Someone had filed off the serial numbers. Only two shots had been fired. With such a cheap revolver, he'd had to have shot her at close range, almost point-blank. There'd probably be some gunshot residue on her face and hand as well. Jack made a mental note to advise Crime Scene, and the ME, then carefully spread open the crumpled-up business card. It was from the Golden Galaxy Karaoke Bar, with a handwritten telephone number scrawled across the back. Jack snapped photos front and back, checked his watch.

6:06 AM.

There was nothing in the man's jacket draped on the chair.

Jack took the note from the man's shirt pocket, and opened it up on the table. The word characters were written out in broken lines, like a Chinese poem, in a Three-Kingdoms-period style. Jack mouthed the words silently, reading through the series of vertical sentences, using his schoolboy Cantonese.

Black Clouds
have covered the sky
like ink.
The whirlwind
sweeps in
from the rivers.
Even the air itself
Is frozen.

Inside,
A growing sorrow
I cannot bear.
There is no one
to turn to,
not even a reflection
in the mirror.

I cannot Face
anyone.
A man
without a face,
I am ready
to do
What I must do . . .

The man had lost face, *mo sai meen*, and had become despondent. A hopeless predicament, according to the poem. Overwhelmed, he'd given in to despair.

Jack pushed back from the table, turned toward the bed. The scene looked like a textbook open-and-shut murder-suicide, one that *any* of the murder squad cops could have stepped up to, way before he'd gotten the call. Even a sergeant and a couple of uniforms could have managed it.

So why me? Jack had to ask himself. Because I'm Chinese? Not that he was complaining. Murder was murder, any way you colored it.

Still.

He went back down the stairs to where the uniformed rookie was leaning against the wall of the little vestibule, half-nodding his way toward the end of the overnight shift. The cold draft of air at the door invigorated Jack.

"What's the deal with Crime Scene?" he asked.

"Sarge said they were en route."

"What about the ME?" Jack frowned. "I need a wagon here."

"I'll notify the sarge *again*."

Jack took a deep gulp of the cold air before quickstepping back upstairs. Inside the apartment, he emptied the woman's handbag onto the linoleum floor. There was nothing unusual: cell phone, makeup, change purse, pen, eyeglasses. A wallet, containing a photo of herself with a karaoke microphone in her hand, smiling; various credit cards, and a non-driver's license that identified her as May Lon Fong, thirty-one years old. Another photo of her with two infants; scrawled across the back of the photo, the Chinese words *ma, jai neui,* mother and children.

The refrigerator was stocked for a single person: two bricks of tofu, some *gai choy,* vegetables, and a gallon jug of *dao jeung*, bean milk. There were leftover salad greens, a half-dozen eggs, a piece of flank steak, dumplings, and noodles in the freezer.

Jack sat down at the little table and waited for the coroner's wagon. Crime Scene would arrive soon enough. Nobody here was going anywhere. The waiting made him wonder again why he'd caught the case, and reminded him of all the Chinatown events that had led up to his recent transfer from the Fifth Precinct. The adrenaline had begun to ebb from his body. Fatigue slowly crept back in.

He remembered how, seven months earlier, he'd gotten a hardship transfer out of Anti-Crime, to be closer to Pa in Chinatown, who'd been terminally ill. The transfer had brought Jack back to the 0-Five, back to the old neighborhood, where he'd grown up, where he'd lost boyhood friends and his innocence, and from which he'd thought he'd finally escaped.

The old man had died recently, and Jack's grief and guilt were still fresh in his heart. He'd moved out on Pa, but only because Chinatown was no longer the same place for him as it was for his father. Jack's Chinatown was colored by violence, death, and a feeling of helplessness that he hated.

He'd become a cop, thinking he'd make a difference. The difference was he'd become as cynical and hard as the gangboys he'd left behind.

He was on the job, working Canal Street with the Anti-Crime plainclothes squad, when Pa passed away. Jack had found him, after stopping to pick up *jook*, congee, for the old man, after the day shift. He'd missed the chance to say good-bye, to try and apologize for the clashes they'd had. And now Jack was the last man standing in the Yu bloodline. Two hundred years of family history on the edge, in *Mei Kwok*, America.

Not long after the burial, a Chinatown tong big shot had gotten himself murdered. Jack was given the case. Uncle Four, leader of the Hip Chings, had been shot coming out of an elevator at 444 Hester Street. One man was in custody, awaiting trial. Another suspect had vanished.

During the investigation, Jack had been suspended by Internal Affairs, but still managed to bring back from San Francisco's Chinatown a New York limousine driver whose name was Johnny *"Wong Jai"* Wong. A person of interest, a Hong Kong Chinese woman, was still at large. They knew her only as Mona.

The case was pending trial.

Johnny Wong's name brought back memories: a short heavyset body lying on the floor, halfway out of a small elevator, the doors bumping up against his ample waist. The vic was Uncle Four. Someone had popped a couple of .25-caliber hi-vels into the back of his head.

Jack had followed Mona's words, her phone tips to him, to California. But when he arrested Johnny Wong for the murder, Johnny, in turn, had pointed the finger at Mona, Fat Uncle's mistress.

Now Johnny was in a cell in Rikers, still claiming he had been framed.

Jack remembered chasing a woman, thirty yards distant, a gun in her hand, desperately pulling a rolling carry-all behind her. She'd escaped from that San Francisco roof-top and disappeared.

Jack knew he'd have to testify to that. So far, none of the Wanteds they'd put out on her had come back, but they had Johnny and the murder weapon, with his prints on it. Sooner or later, the case was going to have its day in court.

Jack recalled the picture of Hong Kong songstress Shirley Yip, torn from *Star! Entertainment,* a Chinese magazine. It was the closest likeness they had of Mona; according to Lucky she was a dead ringer for the celebrity.

Toward the end of his tour in the Fifth, Jack had bumped up against his boyhood friend Tat "Lucky" Louie, who'd tried to recruit him into the ranks of dirty cops on the On Yee tong's payroll. Lucky would have known about the Golden Galaxy, a karaoke dive that was operating on his turf. But Lucky was only being kept alive now by a respirator at Downtown CCU; he'd been caught in a gangland shoot-out between disgruntled Ghost Legion factions. The shoot-out had left seven bodies outside Chinatown OTB, and a possible shooter in flight.

Lucky's luck had run out.

Then there was Alex. Alexandra Lee-Chow, Chinatown *activista* lawyer. Pretty and hard-nosed, but with a soft heart. She was going through a bitter yuppie divorce. And she was drifting in and out of alcoholic self-medication, just like he was.

Since they'd known one another, Jack had steered her past a drunk and disorderly charge, and she'd helped him with his Chinatown cases. During bouts of grief and misery, they'd commiserated and become drinking buddies.

Two budding alcoholics working their way up.

Jack noted that he could use Alex's connections in the Administration for Children's Services for the newly orphaned children, as well as Victim's Services. In addition, there was faith-based support for young victims left parentless. The man and his wife were dead, but their children had to be cared for.

The karaoke photo of the woman reminded him vaguely of Mona. She was like a chameleon. From the little popgun she'd squeezed off firecracker shots at him as he chased her across that rooftop.

Then she was gone. "In the wind." He wondered how far she had flown.

The trilling of his cell phone broke his reverie. The number on the readout was one he didn't recognize.

"Detective Yu?" The voice spoke Toishanese, the old Chinatown dialect.

"Yes, who's this?"

"I am the father." The words froze Jack. "Of the dead man."

"You were here earlier," said Jack.

"Yes, I found the"—a hesitation—"*Say see*, the bodies . . ."

"Sir, I need to speak with you," Jack said in dialect.

"We can meet with you. About half an hour."

"We?" Jack asked.

"Myself," the voice answered, "and the father of the dead woman."

Jack checked his watch. It was 6:18 AM, dark still, but dawn around the edges. He heard the sounds of Crime Scene arriving outside on the quiet street, the voice of the rookie uniformed cop.

"Where?" Jack asked, rechecking his watch.

He left CSU to their work and canvassed the adjacent apartments. The neighbors had heard nothing. No arguments, yelling, sounds of struggle. In the middle of the night, *som gong boon yeh,* they'd been dead asleep.

An old couple in the apartment above heard a bang, but couldn't agree whether there had been one or two. They'd thought it was the street door slamming or the noise of the overnight garbage trucks. Or maybe some *lon jaai,* prankster kids, blasting firecrackers.

He left the building as dawn broke over Chinatown, made a left on Bowery, and headed north toward Canal.

The Nom San Bok Hoy Association was located on the Bowery, north of Hester, past the block of Chinese jewelry stores and the Music Palace Chinese Theater, where the gangboy shoot-outs in the audience were becoming a bigger thrill than the Hong Kong shoot-'em-ups on the big screen.

The Music Palace was becoming obsolete, due to a lively Chinese videotape rental market. Chinese-language entertainment in the comfort of a living room beat a musty, seedy theater hemmed in by perverts, lowlifes, and gangsters. Lucky's Ghosts had fought with both the Dragons and the Yings over this turf.

Why risk your life for a movie?

The Nom San Bok Hoy got its name from landmarks in the villages of the clans who'd emigrated. In their province of the south of China, there were two mountains, one in the north and one in the south. Jack's ancestors traced their lineage to the village of the south mountain, *nom san*. An adjacent village had been located at the north river, *bok hoy*. The villagers got along well and had historically formed alliances. When they arrived in New York's Chinatown, they organized a club, an association for family members and affiliates of their clans. Jack's father had arrived with the third or fourth generation of landed Chinese, a junior member of a small group.

As an association, the Nom San wasn't a big deal, nothing like the Lee Association, or the merchants groups; it had only a couple of hundred members. Jack remembered the Nom San's annual banquets at Port Arthur, a big old-world Chinese restaurant where the kids could play hide-and-seek behind the ornate carved wood panels and banquettes, the tables, and the countertops inlaid with mother of pearl. Chinatown restaurants were now all slick shiny glass and chrome, reflecting the Hong Kong influence, thought Jack. He remembered visiting the association as a child, when Pa, unable to find a babysitter, had brought him along to meetings.

The Nom San building was a five-story walk-up with a rusty redbrick front. Twin flagpoles flew the red, white, and blue banners of both the United States and the Republic of China. Recently, they had rented out the top floor, and had moved the association's meeting hall down to the second floor, above the Fung Wang Restaurant, so that the elders wouldn't have to climb the five flights of stairs to attend a meeting. Outside, there was a red plastic sign, framed in a metallic gold, with shiny yellow letters spelling out the association's name: NOM SAN BOK HOY BENEVOLENT ASSOCIATION. Jack pressed the dusty button at the wire-grated glass door. He was buzzed in immediately, and while ascending the steps, he felt as if they'd been waiting, anticipating his arrival.

At the top of the stairs, he was buzzed in again as he reached for the handle of a gray metal door. Inside was a long open room with bench seating against the side walls. They were sitting at a dark wood table at the far end: two old men he didn't recognize, hunched over, staring into the mahogany surface over clasped hands, as if they were praying. Behind them, against the short back wall, was an old range top, a steaming pot of tea, and a slop sink setup typical of Chinatown in Pa's day. There were racks of folding chairs and tables. A tiny bathroom in the right corner was squeezed in next to a fire-escape exit. Along both long walls, hung on coat pegs above the benches, were folded tray tables. Members had always been welcome to sit and eat their takeout, *hop jaai faahn,* box meals. Displayed higher up on the walls were ancestral plaques and old black-and-white portraits of the village forefathers.

Everything looked flat and sickly under the two rows of fluorescent ceiling lights. The men were both sixtyish, balding. As Jack approached, they raised their frowning faces to him. Their baggy winter clothes and their choked-back grief made them look similar, like relatives, joined by tragedy.

The silence was broken by the rumbling complaint of tractor trailers on the street outside, big trucks navigating the bouncing length of Canal Street, heading toward the Holland Tunnel.

Jack pulled a stool up to the table and sat, showing the gold detective's badge at his waist. He smelled camphor, the scent of *mon gum yao,* tiger balm, and *bok fa yao,* minty oil. The old men had resorted to herbal liniments to help fight off their looming nausea and despair.

The more haggard of the two spoke first. "We appreciate your help," he said. "Ah Gong here remembered your father, Sing *gor.*"

The other man said, "We asked for you because a *tong yen,* Chinese, would be more understanding . . . that this is the saddest day of our lives."

"I respect that," Jack answered. "Who called me?"

"I am *lo* Gong," said the second man. "My son . . . is the dead man. I got your telephone number from the police card that your father had left here."

Jack remembered. He believed that Pa, in his disdain and anger over his son becoming a running dog cop, had discarded his NYPD detective's card. So this murder-suicide case had come his way through his dead father's actions.

Gong removed a driver's license from his wallet, handing it over to Jack.

"Ah *jai,*" he whispered. "My son."

"This is against nature," Fong said. "We are not meant to survive our children."

Jack nodded quietly in agreement. Bitterness and anger choked their voices, two old heads shaking in disbelief: How can this be? Their eyes searched desperately in the middle distance for answers.

The license was expired, but recent enough. The male

shooter had been Harry Gong, thirty-four years old, five feet nine inches in height. He had an address at Grand Street, toward the northern edge of Chinatown.

He looked more like a student than a gangbanger.

There was a pronounced silence in the empty meeting hall, then each of the fathers spoke in turn, spilling out the story of how he reached this . . . end of the world.

"They'd been together five years. Husband and wife," said Gong.

"They have two young children. Two and three years old," added Fong.

"A happy family . . ."

Jack took a deep *shaolin* boxer's breath through his nose. He hated cases where children were involved; those situations gouged at his toughness, fractured the hard shell he'd built around his cop's heart.

He let the men continue in their odd Chinese cadence.

"Then they separated, this year."

"She had a depression. The kind young mothers get."

"He was afraid for the children."

"They had bruises."

"She moved back to her old studio apartment."

"He hoped the situation would get better."

"Then she got a job in a bakery."

"After a few months, she asked for a separation."

"And he agreed, reluctantly."

Neither man had shed a tear but Jack could sense the sadness and anger just beneath the grim masks of their faces.

"She seemed better, and visited the children."

"The doctor at the clinic said these things take time."

"My son continued working long hours. *Kay toy*, waiting tables. At the Wong Sing. He was even more stressed, more nervous than before."

"Our wives and cousins took care of the children."

They paused as if to catch their breaths, Jack sensing the darkening of their tale.

"My daughter changed jobs, worked in a karaoke club. Fewer hours and more money."

"My son found out. He didn't like her working until four in the morning. It wasn't a job for a woman her age."

"She refused to quit."

"He felt he'd lost face. One day he was angry, the next day sad."

"But she said the money was good. And the job was like *freedom*. It made her feel better about herself."

"But he couldn't accept the idea of the club. Drinking and singing all night. The kind of people who went there . . ."

"She denied any involvements. She said she was only saving for her future and the children's future."

"They had a big argument."

"Several weeks ago."

"He begged her to quit."

"But she refused again."

"Did he threaten her?" Jack interrupted.

"It wasn't his nature," Gong answered.

"He kept it all inside," from Fong.

"Did they get help? Seek counseling?" Jack asked.

"They're both grown-ups, both thirty-something years old."

"We felt they would work it out."

"And you never saw this coming?" Jack challenged.

Both men shook their heads. No, no never, was followed by uneasy silence.

Seizing the moment, Jack slipped in a question, catching them off guard. "Where did he get the gun?"

Another dead pause, then both men answered in unison, "We don't know."

Jack let the moment drift, looking for some effect, but was met with only their gnarled stone faces.

"I didn't see any sign of forced entry," Jack offered.

"He had a key," Fong said.

"From when they were dating," added Gong.

He was waiting for her, Jack remembered thinking.

"What brought you to the scene?" he asked Gong.

"I've had trouble sleeping," Gong answered. "So I was in the kitchen when my son left the apartment."

"What time was this?"

"Three something, close to four o'clock." Gong clenched and unclenched his fists, heartbreak working its way out despite his arthritis. "I asked where he was going *som gong boon yeh*, in the middle of the night? 'For a walk,' he said. 'It's freezing,' I told him. But he said he needed the air. I waited half an hour, then I called his *sau gay*, cell phone, but got no answer. Then I went to look for him."

"Why didn't you call the police then?" quizzed Jack.

"And tell them what? I never thought something like this might happen."

"So you went to her place?"

"I went to the singing club first, but it was already closed.

Then I went to Doyers Street. I called his cell phone again, from the hallway. I could hear his ringtone from inside but it just kept ringing. I have a key, and let myself in." He began to tremble and nervously massaged his twisted fingers.

"Ah Gong called me at about five AM," interjected Fong. "I drove in from New Jersey. Almost an hour and a half, sitting in traffic. I didn't know the rush hour started so early. I wanted to jump from the car and run to Chinatown."

"I saw the bodies," Gong continued. "I knew they were dead. But I couldn't stay inside. I could feel their *gwai*— ghosts—in there. I felt I might go insane so I went into the hallway. I called the association's secretary and asked him to call the police, to ask for you, *lo* Yu."

"Who did he call, exactly?" asked Jack.

"I don't know. He said he would take care of it."

Jack took a breath and rose off the stool slowly, looking toward the dim daylight streaming in through the dirty picture windows. He'd have to go to the station house, see what the captain had on this.

Gong said, "We need to be strong."

Fong agreed. "For the two families to survive. The women will become hysterical."

"You haven't told them?" Jack asked, quietly stunned.

"We are . . . preparing to . . . tell them. It isn't natural, you see. How do we go on now?"

"*Jing deng,*" Gong said fatalistically. "It's destiny."

The Chinese, Jack knew, attributed acts of incomprehensible evil to destiny, *jing deng*, believing that things were meant to be, that there was nothing they could have done to prevent it. Self-absolution.

"Detective," Fong said, "we hope we can depend on your discretion. In case of gossip, or rumors."

"Rumors?" Jack lifted an eyebrow. "Like what?"

"Someone may say she was a hostess, a *siu jeer,* in the ka-la-ok. But she was a manager," Fong insisted, "not a hostess. The newspapers, you know they like to make up stories."

"There should not be any more shame attached to this story," Gong added.

"I understand," Jack said. Finally, there it was again, the reason for Jack being here: the ever-present Chinese concern about saving face, about the loss of face, fear of scandalous speculation, dishonor to their children, to their families, to themselves.

The fathers stood up, steeling themselves for the grim task ahead, delivering the tragic news to their families, each old man barely able to contain his heartbreak.

Jack wrote down their phone numbers.

"I may need you to come down to the station house later."

"We have to make the funeral arrangements. We will be in Chinatown."

It was 7:45 AM when Jack stepped back into the raw cold daylight of the Bowery, heading south toward Elizabeth Alley and the Fifth Precinct station house. Along the way, he stopped at Me Lee Snack and got a steaming cup of *nai cha,* tea with milk, watching the patrol cars roll in and out of Elizabeth Alley, hoping that the captain was an early bird and had already arrived.

The 0-Five house was the oldest in the city, a run-down

Federalist brick-front walk-up built in 1881, just before the Chinese Exclusion Acts, when the area was known as the notorious Five Points, home to mostly Irish and Italians and a scattering of other European ethnicities.

Jack remembered the beat-up metal desk in the second-floor squad room where he'd worked the Uncle Four murder, and later, the Ghost Legion shoot-out.

Both cases were still open, investigations continuing.

Captain Salvatore "Big Sal" Marino was the CO, commanding officer of the Fifth Precinct. Jack remembered well all five months of the troublesome tour he'd previously served under Marino, during which more things went wrong than right.

In spite of that, Jack had gotten the job done, and the captain had personally quashed a subsequent Internal Affairs investigation. Later, Marino had quietly pushed for Jack's promotion to Detective Second Grade.

In his stuffy office, the captain stood beside his big wooden desk, nodding his white-haired head as he said, "Homicide-suicide, open and shut. That's what the watch sarge said."

"Looks that way," agreed Jack. "The ME's got them now."

"When they're done, wrap it up. You can use your old desk in the squad room."

Great, thought Jack sardonically, thanks a lot.

The captain gave Jack a puzzled look, grinned, then said, "You're wondering why you, hah? It's not like we didn't have homicide cops available, right?" He straightened up from the desk, let his bulk loom toward Jack, and spoke in a confessional tone. "The call came down from

Manhattan South." He took a breath. "A PBA rep phoned the night watch. Then an accommodation came down the chain, *capisce?* They need a Chinese cop? Sure, why not? This group, wassit? The Nom San? Made a generous donation to the Widows and Orphans Fund last year. Some of their members are auxiliaries, volunteer police. So why not? They're good fellas, right?" He put a hammy hand on Jack's shoulder, saying, "So here you are."

And here I am, thought Jack. Back in the 'hood.

"It's not the usual procedure," Marino continued. "But if the *community* feels a *Chinese* detective might be more sensitive to the investigation, I'm inclined to be accommodating."

Jack mused, Always alert to an opportunity for some good PR. Of course the precinct was ready to cooperate with the skeptical community, especially for street information relating to the safety (gangs and guns) and security (extortion and gambling, drugs and prostitution) of the people of Chinatown. Always ready. CPR. Courtesy, Professionalism, Respect.

"Accommodating is good," Jack agreed, fighting off a sneer.

"Exactly. Survivors don't want bullshit finding its way into the newspapers." He paused. "Especially with the Chinese press being what it is."

"How's that, Captain?" Jack asked, sensing racism. Jack remembered Vincent Chin, editor of the *United National,* Chinatown's oldest newspaper. Vincent had assisted Jack in past investigations.

"Look, just be *sensitive,* hah?" Marino warned. "Obviously, they didn't want to talk to a *gwailo,* a white cop."

Sensitivity, Jack thought, was like diversity, affirmative action, and equal opportunity: convenient catchwords that people in command used to cover their asses.

"You work the paperwork any way you want," Marino advised. "But I'm gonna be reading in between the lines. And you better be sure everything's *straight*, by the book. You get my drift?"

"Right, Captain," Jack answered. "I'll keep you posted."

"Do that," the big man said, checking his watch. "And stay in the neighborhood. ADA Sing's coming by at nine thirty."

Jack knew that prosecutor Bang Sing, a rising young star in the DA's office, was also a friend of Alexandra's.

"You'll need his updates on the Johnny Wong case," said Marino, tilting his head dismissively toward the open door.

"Nine thirty, yes sir," acknowledged Jack. There was an hour and a half in between.

Jack went right on Bayard, left on Mott, thinking of Billy Bow and the Tofu King, which was across the street from the Golden Galaxy club where May Lon Fong had worked. He continued past the dingy storefronts of his childhood, toward the billowing cloud of steam that rushed forth every time a customer exited the Tofu King. It had once been Chinatown's biggest tofu distributor, but in recent decades, it had seen its fortunes decline in the face of cutthroat competition and rising costs. The Bows had resorted to promotional gimmicks to stem their loss of market share. Half-price early-bird deals for senior citizens. Leftover "value packs" after 6 PM. Three generations of a longtime Chinatown family, the Bows were hanging on against fierce Fukienese competition from East Broadway and the growth of the health-foods industry.

Billy Bow, the only son, was Jack's oldest friend, his last *hingdaai,* brother, in the neighborhood, the one who hadn't cut and run for the suburbs, who hadn't fallen victim to gangs, drugs, or to the shakedowns that came from the tongs, or to the various taxes imposed by municipal thieves as well.

Jack had worked in the Tofu King for three years, lost years, between the military and college and his job with the NYPD.

Billy was Jack's extra ears and eyes on the street, and had a merchant's insight into the tribal and political workings of the neighborhood. More than a few violent incidents had led back to business deals gone bad, and merchants were known to be involved with gambling cash and contraband deals.

Jack stepped through the steam into the humid shop and saw Billy in the back area with the slop boys. He scooped up plastic containers of *dao foo fa,* tofu custard, and *bok tong go,* a gelatinous dessert, and headed for the cashier, but Billy noticed him right away.

"*Wai waiwai!*" Billy yelled to the cashier, waving off Jack's dollars. "His *chien*'s no good here!"

"Come on, Billy." Jack shook his head. "You gotta stop doing this."

"*Fuhgeddaboudit,* hah? Start the new year off right."

"Thanks," Jack said resignedly, "like always." He pocketed his money and glanced out the fogged window to the other side of the street.

"What happened?" Billy grinned. "You back in the shit?"

"Nah," Jack frowned, "just wrapping up a case." He

27

nodded in the direction of the yellow Golden Galaxy kara-oke sign. "What's going on down there these days?"

"Karaoke?" puzzled Billy. "Same buncha kids hanging out in front all the time. Noisy as hell. Leave their garbage all over the fuckin' street. And you know I can't sing worth a shit."

Jack laughed, letting Billy run on.

"So I only been down there once or twice. But five bucks for a beer and ten dollars for a *lo mein?* Fuhgeddaboudit. Rip-off. But then I heard the Ghosts are dealing bags and pills out of there. Probably you-know-what-else, too."

Jack understood that to mean heroin, China White. "What kind of crowd?" he asked, thinking of May Lon Fong.

"They're like a young Hong Kong crowd," Billy pondered, "but they got snakehead *nui,* smuggled girls, hustling off the big beers, brandy, and bar food. Probably got tong cash backing the place."

The Ghosts, thought Jack. He considered paying a visit during the late hours but knew the Ghosts would make him right away, even if he played his way in with Alexandra on his arm. Two romantics out for a singsong.

"Ghosts," sneered Billy. "Fuhgeddaboudit. The girls don't last long there before getting dirty."

Exactly the kind of innuendo that the victims' families didn't want, thought Jack.

Billy was another bad influence, another brick in Jack's protective wall around his feelings, fortifying his skeptical view of relationships, pushing him to keeping Alex at a distance.

"That's how bitches are," Billy complained. "They fuck around when they think they can get over."

Billy, the bitter divorcé, was protective of his heart, but was a weekly regular at Angelina Chao's pussy palace, where only matters of his cock were involved.

"Why?" Billy asked. "Somebody kill somebody with their sorry-ass singing?"

"Nah." Jack laughed. "I just need some background for the paperwork."

Billy lit up a cigarette. "This kid, Jing Zhang, moonlights down there, after slopping beans here."

"I might need to speak to him," said Jack.

"Too early. He's probably splitting some young Fukienese flower right about now." He checked his beat-up Swatch watch. "Come back after ten."

"Thanks," Jack offered as they pounded fists.

"Later."

Jack left the Tofu King, swinging his little red plastic bag of Chinese desserts, and went toward Division Street, a freezing winter wind tunnel. He lowered his head to the steady, relentless wind, until he passed beneath the Manhattan Bridge onto Allen, leading out past the Chrystie Street park where the local needleheads once ruled, sharing shots and hatching up their junkie schemes of the day.

The Loisaida side streets blended into NoHo, until he came to a big yellow banner over a storefront that used to be a bodega. The yellow banner proclaimed ASIAN AMERICAN JUSTICE ADVOCACY, or AJA, pronounced Asia.

AJA had begun as a grassroots activist organization staffed by young lawyers and law students fighting for positive change, paying back the community with pro

29

bono time. The gritty feeling of the neighborhood made him wonder if Alexandra had visited the pistol range he'd suggested. He'd helped her to get a pistol permit when she'd been spooked by phone threats the AJA had received for aiding runaways smuggled in by the snakeheads. Alex had purchased a .22-caliber revolver, a Smith & Wesson Ladysmith.

Pausing at the door, Jack viewed the storefront operation that was a jumble of used office furniture and donated equipment. It was too easy to see inside, and because of AJA's proximity to the avenues of Alphabet City, there were groups of homeless men loitering nearby who appeared sinister and threatening.

There was no one at the reception desk. He saw Alex through the small pane of glass in the wood door. She was in her late twenties but could still pass for an undergrad. She was sitting and watching some news footage on the little color TV by her desk.

Alex saw Jack enter, nodded, and resumed watching the TV. He knew it was a tape when she rewound the images back across the screen before turning off the set. Jack remembered that the same crime scenes and follow-up footage had been shown by the media extensively during the week.

Four days earlier there'd been a shooting in Queens: an officer had responded to a call and encountered a teenager playing with a pellet gun. In the ensuing struggle, the teenager was shot in the back of the head and died.

The Chinese teenager was an honor student and the officer was a second-year rookie. The case had taken an abrupt turn when the report from the Medical Examiner's office concluded that the path of the fatal police bullet didn't support the NYPD claim that it was an accidental shooting.

Internal Affairs was all over the scenario now, as was the Queens DA's office.

The media was having a field day with it.

"The funeral's today," Alex said quietly, "but one of the uncles is screaming 'wrongful death.'"

Jack knew that to mean a lawsuit was imminent but remained quiet because he'd seen the controversy coming. Wrongful police actions made him feel awkward, but he knew it was inevitable; on a force of thirty thousand men and women, there was bound to be some unfortunate incidents. It wasn't the first time Alex had taken the Chinese side against the NYPD, and although she didn't direct any of her contempt for bad cops toward Jack personally, he still caught her negative thoughts directed at his gun and shield.

"And I can't do it," Alex added.

Jack gave her a puzzled look.

"I've got two cases already," she continued. "Plus I'll be in Seattle during the hearings."

"Seattle?" asked Jack.

"The CADS are invited to ORCA's annual awards gala," Alex said distractedly.

CADS was the Chinese-American Defense Squad, Alex's clever little acronym for her group of eight Chinese lawyers, a judge, and a half-dozen paralegal misfits who nevertheless knew how to make the system sing. They'd taken on some police brutality beefs and a few controversial discrimination cases, and had won convincingly.

ORCA was the Organization for Rights of Chinese-Americans, a civil-rights organization that had eighty-eight chapters nationwide. They'd supported legal actions following the much-publicized "mistaken identity" murder of a young Chinese man in 1982 in Detroit.

"Death by cop," said Alex, frowning. "They kill you for pulling out a wallet. Or a cell phone, or a *hairbrush*. Everything looks like a gun."

"From what I'm hearing, it was a good shoot," Jack reluctantly offered.

"*Good?*" Her eyes narrowed. "He shot the kid in the head while restraining him. How can that be good?"

"You know what I mean," Jack said evenly. "They say the arrest was textbook, just—"

"Only the 'gun' didn't follow the textbook, huh?" She looked away.

Jack shrugged. This was an argument he didn't want any part of.

"He was a straight-A kid, Jack," said Alex, unrelenting, "the kind of kid every parent wishes their child could be." She sighed, and there was an awkward silence between them.

He'd chosen a bad time to visit but was glad he was able to bring something sweet into Alex's frustrating and melancholy morning. He surprised her by setting the bag of Tofu King desserts on her desk, and saw her face brighten momentarily.

"I'm not sure how to take this," she said, opening one of the plastic containers of *bok tong go*.

"How's that?" puzzled Jack.

"Well, the only time you come out here," she said as she bit into one of the spongy white sweets, "is when something bad brings you to Chinatown."

Jack took a deep breath. He was silent a moment while the images of a dead Chinese couple did a jump cut in his mind.

"What is it this time?" Alex asked, her big eyes cautiously looking up at him.

Abruptly, Jack asked, "What do you think about post-partum depression?"

"Excuse me?" she said as she leaned back in her chair.

"I mean here, in Chinatown," Jack explained. "Among Chinese-speaking immigrants? Do they believe in it? Or get treatment for it?"

Alex realized Jack wasn't kidding. "Well, the younger generation knows about it. The health clinic distributes brochures in Chinese. And they have outreach programs."

"And the older generation?" He watched her finish off the sweet. "Do they dismiss it? Like it's a myth?"

Alex leaned forward and folded her arms across the top of her desk. Jack glanced away to avoid staring at the soft curves of her cleavage.

"The old folks have a traditional spin on it," she said. "They use herbs and soups. Certain foods to rebalance the mother's body, knowing how the body and mind are linked."

"Right," Jack realized. "An unbalanced mind explains why a mother might hurt her own children."

Alex studied Jack's face before asking, "You're here on behalf of dead children again?"

"No," he answered. "Just looking for some clarity. . . ." He wanted to change the subject. "So, you ever make it down to the pistol range?"

The thought of guns sobered her, brought her back to the realities of crime on these Lower East Side streets.

"Twice," she answered.

"How'd it go?"

"I'm a regular Annie Oakley now, okay?"

"Yeah, right." Jack grinned.

Her desk phone rang and Jack waved good-bye to her as she took the call. He was thinking about the big police captain, the Chinese prosecutor Bang Sing, and the disposable camera in his pocket as he left the storefront.

When he got back to Chinatown, Ah Fook's Thirty-Minute Photo had just opened. Jack gave the camera to Fook junior, who would print the film before processing the other orders of the morning. Jack would pick it up later, after checking in with Billy Bow.

Law and Order

ADA Bang Sing reminded Jack of a younger Chow Yun-Fat, Hong Kong's John Wayne. He wore a black coat over a black suit and had a well-traveled, cosmopolitan air about him. Captain Marino leaned back in his big chair and let him talk.

"The judge set bail at a million dollars," Sing said in an urbane voice, "because of the flight risk. But he's really interested in seeing who's going to step up for Johnny." Sing paused for effect. "So far, no takers."

Jack and Marino traded glances and the ADA continued, "So far there's no action on his remand. He's cooling his ass at Rikers and there's no requirement of a 'speedy trial' in a murder case." Again, he paused for effect. "Sheldon Littman's the lawyer for Johnny, and he waived the grand jury. They're claiming they need time for discovery as to who this woman of interest is, because she turns up in your testimony."

Again Jack flashed back to the running shoot-out across the San Francisco Chinatown rooftop, and the petite woman with short hair who was squeezing off .25-caliber slugs at him.

"Meanwhile," Sing continued, "Johnny's had visitors. Chinese men who claim to be Hong Kong affiliates of Littman's. They said Johnny's testimony needs a better translation than that of a regular court appointee, because of his limited English. And Littman's trying to get Johnny moved to softer digs. Maybe an empty federal squat."

Jack remembered Mona's tape-recorded words, implicating Johnny.

"So here's the deal," Sing said as if in a summation. "When we go to trial, the existence of this woman is going to create doubt about Johnny being the lone shooter. They're going to work *you* over on cross-examination. And we need to limit the damage."

"Bullshit," Jack said quietly.

"Minimum, we still get him for conspiracy to commit murder, aiding and abetting a homicide. Littman's going to paint Johnny as a hapless fuckhead who fell for this missing woman. And then got suckered." Another pause. "With *your* testimony, there's enough he can play on to support that."

"More bullshit," said Jack with a sneer.

"There's a big chill on right now," Sing advised. "But I'll keep you posted."

"Thanks." Jack smiled sardonically.

After the ADA left, Jack pulled the Wanted posters from the open case files. A file that Jack had labeled EDDIE NG/ SHORTY contained a juvenile offender mugshot of Keung "Eddie" Ng, who Jack believed was involved in the Ghost Legion OTB shoot-out that had left six dead, and Lucky in a coma. The photo was ten years old; a baby-faced kid who'd probably looked different now.

He took out a Wanted poster bearing the Shirley Yip image from Mona's file and pocketed both. He would visit Billy Bow and the Fuk kid. After, Jack thought, he'd look for Ah Por, the old wise woman he knew, to see if she had any clues for him.

At the Tofu King, the Fuk kid, Jing Zhang, recognized the karaoke photo of May Lon Fong that Jack had taken from her wallet. Zhang was leery about Jack the Chinese cop but Billy said, "It's okay, JZee, he's *good* police."

Zhang relaxed, saying in broken Cantonese, "She kept to herself. She was old for that crowd."

"Did she seem happy?" Jack asked. "Or was someone bothering her?"

Zhang frowned and shrugged his shoulders at the word "happy." "The manager"—he glanced at Billy—"he's a Ghost. He had his pick of the women. And there were the gang girls, always flirting with him." He paused, scanned the store floor nervously. "But I never saw anything between him and her. Like I said, she was kind of old for him."

"What time did she get off work?" Jack continued.

"Four thirty, mostly."

"In the morning."

"That's right."

"And she closed the club?"

Jing chortled. "The Ghosts close the club. They let her out a few minutes before they locked the gates."

A dangerous time of night, thought Jack. But at least she lived nearby. Two blocks from Doyers Street. The few minutes it'd take for her to get home would be the last moments she'd have had to herself before encountering her ex-husband.

"What else?" Jack asked.

"That's *it*. I'm in the kitchen most of the time."

Jack dismissed the kid to his work, and Billy accompanied him to the back area, where they started slopping the beans.

After he left the Tofu King, Jack headed for the Senior Citizen Center, on a hunch that the old wise woman, Ah Por, would be there. Normally, Ah Por kept company with the groups of elderly fortune-telling women who gathered in Columbus Park, but the freezing weather prohibited that now. More than likely she'd be at the center, finishing off her bowl of congee, served free to senior citizens. Jack remembered her from the times Pa had brought him to visit the old woman, with her red book and cup of sticks, seeking lucky words, or numbers, or good news. This was after Ma died. Jack never forgot. He'd been a young child, and didn't remember much of his mother.

More recently, Ah Por's readings provided accurate if oblique clues for Jack, helping in his investigations. He found her in the back of the lunchroom, in a sea of old heads, listening to the Chung Wah Chinese Broadcasting's radio program that was being played over the PA system.

"Ah Por," Jack said, just loud enough to catch her ear, to make her glance up at him, a glint of recognition in her old eyes. He didn't see any of her tools of divination but he knew she also applied "face reading" to everyday items, using them to channel with an eerie clairvoyant's touch.

"Ah Por," Jack repeated, handing her the photo of May Lon Fong and the expired driver's license of Harry Gong. He pressed a folded five-dollar bill into her rheumatic hand, smiled, and bowed his head.

Ah Por ran a thumb over the smiling face of the woman in the photograph, over the karaoke microphone she held. She repeated the moves over the man's face on the driver's license. She pocketed the money and closed her eyes.

Jack remembered that she spoke softly, and leaned in closer.

"She is a snake."

Huh? thought Jack.

"And he is a pig," she added, her eyes snapping open. Dementia? considered Jack.

"They are incompatible. Better is the Snake with an Ox, or a Rooster."

Jack realized she was referring to the animals in the Chinese zodiac.

"She is Fire, and he is Water," Ah Por continued. "Worlds apart." She paused, and shook her head. "He is still in love with her. But she is full with bitterness."

Ah Por handed Jack back the photo and license.

"Their union can come to no good end."

"Thank you," Jack said, handing her the two posters from the open case files, slipping another five into her hand. She pocketed the money and held the Wanted posters apart, one in each hand. She swept her fingers across each of the faces, slowly rolling her head.

Jack leaned closer.

Lifting up the poster of Eddie Ng, Ah Por said, "*Yuh*," meaning rain, followed by, "*Lo mok*," Cantonese slang for *Negro*.

Jack noted Ah Por's responses, although he continued to puzzle over their meaning.

From the second poster, the magazine photo likeness of Mona, Ah Por said *yuh* again. Is she confused? wondered Jack. She gave him a faraway look, adding, "*Seui*," water.

"Water over water," she concluded, handing him back the posters.

Jack thanked her again, wondering if it was all mystical mumbo-jumbo meant to torment him, another Chinatown curse.

Ah Por cackled, turned, and walked away, patting her money pocket, her signal to Jack that the session was over. He watched her disappear into the crowd of ancient folks milling about, their voices blending together amidst the sounds of Chinese radio.

The smell of congee had made him think of the Wong Sing Restaurant, where Harry Gong had worked. Jack decided to go along Columbus Park. He passed the string of Chinese funeral parlors that lined the street opposite the playgrounds and ballfields of the park side: the Chao Funeral House, the Wah Fook Parlor, the Sun Wing Parlor, the Wing Ching Parlor. Jack saw the large white tickets prominently posted on the glass doors of the parlor's entrances; each ticket bore a Chinese ink-brushed name, each black on white ticket representing a deceased person.

There were eight tickets at the Wah Fook. Eight also at the Sun Wing. The Chao had posted six, and the Wing Ching, five. The funeral drivers would work double shifts this week.

Twenty-seven bodies leaving Mulberry Street, heading toward everlasting peace.

January and February were the cruelest months, Jack thought, with the deadly flu season and the subzero cold picking off the elderly and the infirm. At least two dozen deaths a week during these winter months. And they'd be receiving two more bodies quick enough, Jack knew, as soon as the Medical Examiner was done with May Lon Fong and Harry Gong.

Jack cut left to Mosco Street, then left again to Pell, and saw the place he sought a short distance up the street. The Wong Sing Restaurant featured home-style Cantonese dishes, with a side wall of quickie takeout: *ningjouh,* or *haang gaai,* "food walking" containers of chopped chicken, duck, or roast pork over rice, topped with a fried egg. Two countermen worked a range top where soup noodles cooked, and plated the various combinations.

There were eight small tables that could be arranged together. No tablecloths. Three waiters loitered around a shelf station filled with glasses and pots of tea. It was early enough for Jack to be their first customer, but this was a late breakfast for him. He ordered *pei don jook,* thousand-year-egg congee, with a *yow jow gwai,* fried cruller, that made for a hot, slurpy, and filling meal.

One of the waiters brought him a steaming glass of brown tea.

Jack drafted notes for the reports that he knew Captain Marino would ask for, then he observed the waiters between spoonfuls of *jook.* He thought about Harry Gong and his days as a waiter here.

Typically, Chinatown waiters worked a ten- to twelve-hour day, five, sometimes six days a week. The bulk of their take-home pay consisted of tips, which everyone underreported. The Wong Sing was a small restaurant, and no one here was making enormous tips like the waiters in the large banquet-style restaurants. The full-time waiters could take off an hour or two between the lunch and dinner shifts, between 3:30 and 5:30 PM. Those who lived close enough could do their errands, spend time with their families, or make a

41

quick run to OTB. The part-time waiters covered the full shift and helped the kitchen staff prepare vegetables during the dead hours.

The Wong Sing waiters laughed among themselves at an inside joke, and Jack understood their camaraderie. They'd spend more time here with their coworkers, their "brothers," than they did with their loved ones. Family life *had* to suffer.

Jack imagined Harry Gong going home to an unhappy wife after twelve hours of waiting tables. He also imagined an exasperated May Lon, after an exhausting day caring for two children, facing a dead-tired *lo gung*, husband, who was deaf to her frustrations.

Jack knew that the demands of work and of parenting often broke families apart. None of the negative kharma he felt reflected well on relationships, fortifying Jack's cynicism.

Collecting his notes, Jack remembered that he needed to see Chinese newspaper editor Vincent Chin, and finished his congee.

He left an extra dollar tip on the way out.

The *United National* was located on White Street, hidden behind the Tombs, a city detention facility, and the rundown building of the Men's Mission. Vincent Chin managed the operation from its renovated storefront inside a converted warehouse building.

·The newspaper had a staff of twenty: pressmen, reporters, and editors. They used freelance photographers and downloaded free graphics. The copy was typeset by layout men who inserted the tiny metal Chinese characters into the press forms by hand.

The *United National* had been Pa's favorite, his hometown newspaper. Its editor had assisted Jack on previous cases in Chinatown by divulging hearsay details, loose street talk, and calls from anonymous tipsters: details that were inadmissible in court, unverifiable, and unprintable in the paper.

Vincent was sipping from a steamy take-out cup of *nai cha* tea when Jack walked into his little office. Jack proceeded to provide Vincent with the particulars of the May Lon Fong and Harry Gong murder-suicide case, sticking to the facts, leaving out the speculation.

Jack was happy to lay out the straight scoop for Vincent, knowing he would write the true story, and that the other Chinese dailies would have to follow suit if they wanted timely coverage. When Jack finished, he said, "But you know the deal. Don't print it until the department okays it. You could probably add it late to tomorrow's issue."

Vincent nodded in agreement and said, "Call me," smiling his Chinese Chesire-cat smile as Jack left his office.

Jack picked up his crime scene snapshots from Ah Fook's and brought them back to the station house. He spread them across the desk and they brought back the scene. Dead hands together, in lifeless passage, the expressions on the faces of the deceased recalling the enormity of the killings, the color snapshots freezing the agony of their tragedy.

Jack stayed away from the emotional edge of it, setting out only the facts in his paperwork. He felt like a drink, but before he realized it, it was mid-afternoon. He left the paperwork on the captain's desk, a neat overview awaiting only the ME and CSU reports. Included in the file were his quickie snapshots.

He came back to the squad room, where his attention wandered to the array of items he'd shown to Ah Por, still puzzling over the clues she'd given him.

Rain?

Water over water?

Lo mok?

They were hidden explanations, cloaked in yellow witch-craft and Taoist mysticism.

Mona. He remembered her voice, her words spoken in flight, accusing limo driver Johnny Wong of murdering Uncle Four. Mona. The fat man's mistress, now a shadow in the wind.

Rain? Water Over Water?

Was Eddie Ng a *lo mok,* a *Negro?*

None of it made sense now but Jack's experience was that all of it would tie in later, somehow.

He was about to step away from his desk when the old man entered the squad room. One of the uniforms pointed Mr. Fong, May Lon's father, in Jack's direction. Surprised to see him, Jack offered him a chair. The victim's father sat and took a deep sighing breath.

"The families know now," he explained, staring down at the worn linoleum floor. "I've come from the Wah Fook," he said, shaking his head in quiet disbelief. "I made all the arrangements."

"It's a terrible thing, *ah bok,*" Jack said solemnly.

Old Fong glanced up at Jack, then again bowed his head toward the floor. Jack figured Fong had remembered things he'd wanted to say earlier, but he'd deferred to the presence of the shooter's father, *lo* Gong; things he'd felt the Chinese detective would understand.

"She is . . . *was* a good daughter," Fong said, "and a hard worker. Before she got married, she always had a job. Always made money, and bought things for the family."

Jack nodded sympathetically. "She honored her parents."

"Very much so." Fong's gaze bore through the floor. "And she was independent. Traveled all over." He wrung his hands. "Then she got married." His voice was tinged with regret.

Jack had heard the flipside already, a cynical scenario that again didn't bode well for his own thoughts about marriage and family in this screwed-up modern age.

"May Lon didn't like depending on her husband for money. She wasn't used to the demands of young children, or being cooped up indoors all day. She'd felt isolated. Her husband was away at work most of the time. Her sadness grew deeper and darker. The pressure got to her. The clinic's brochures explained it, but we never did find the right Chinese words for postpartum depression."

Fong rubbed his temples, hunched his shoulders. "We never reported her *beng*, her illness. Everyone was afraid they would take away the children," he said, drawing another deep breath. "Instead, she moved out. When she started working again, she seemed happy. She seemed happy when she visited the children."

The karaoke job had been her salvation, but had brought only humiliation and anger to her husband. Ah Por had read their faces correctly: they were incompatible, like Fire and Water. Mix them together and you got tragedy.

"Husband said the *sai louh*, the little ones, needed their mother. We offered to watch the children full time," Fong continued, "but husband was against it. Seniors, *lo yun ga*, should enjoy their golden years, he argued, not hassle with small children. What could we say to that?"

Jack could see the man's eyes start to glisten, his grief rising to the surface, but the tears never flowed. He'd hide them inside until he got to family time, until after the funeral, after the burial. Then and thereafter, his tears would be eternal.

Fong rose from the chair and stared into the last of the afternoon light outside the squad-room window. His gaze finally came back to Jack, and with a nod of his head and a small wave of his hand, he said, "Thank you for your help. Your father was a good man, and raised a good son," and turned away.

Jack watched him go down the stairs and out of the station house.

It was already dark when one of the uniforms from the evening shift dropped off the Medical Examiner's report. Jack reviewed it along with the Crime Scene Unit's.

The comparative reports confirmed the scenario Jack had envisioned: May Lon had arrived home, was surprised by Harry, was made to sit at the edge of the bed, and was shot shortly after. The Medical Examiner indicated COD, cause of death, as a GSW, a gunshot wound, through the frontal bone of the cranium, exiting via the back of the skull. CSU had found the twisted little slug behind the bed.

The kill shot was angled downward, indicating Harry must have been standing over her. Traces of gunshot residue, GSR, were found on her palm and on her face as well, which meant Harry was less than two feet away when he fired.

Was he talking to her? Pleading?

The wound in her right hand was a neat little round hole in her palm that extended through it, as if she'd thrown up the hand to ward off the bullet.

Did he show her the poem? Did he read it to her?

So the .22-caliber hi-vel slug had torn through her hand before blasting into her forehead and skull, then crashed around, ripping up cerebrum and cerebellum before exiting the middle back her head, slamming her into the hereafter.

The amount of blood that seeped into the comforter indicated she'd bled out over a short time, but the high-velocity gunshot wound to the head had probably killed her instantly. The ME listed approximate time of death—expiration—as 4:30 to 4:40 AM.

The broken clock radio on the linoleum floor, stopped at 4:44 AM. The shooter hadn't waited long. The desperate, despondent note poem in his pocket. Not long before he ate the gun.

According to CSU, the shooter had lowered his mouth over the gun barrel, his head bowed as if in prayer, when he pulled the trigger. The bullet bored through the top of his mouth, tumbled, and blew his brains out of the top left side of his head. He had GSR on his right hand, the gun hand. Also, some GSR stippling on his face and mouth area. Consistent with the murder-suicide scenario.

They'd likely match Harry's fingerprints to the gun and the shell casings.

The ME listed the manner of death as DOMESTIC DISPUTE: estranged husband shoots ex-wife, then self, in double tragedy. Two children left behind.

Jack began to feel the weight of the early morning: fourteen hours on the job, the emotional drag of the case.

He really needed a drink.

He could see the Chinatown darkness outside the captain's windows as he placed the reports on the desk in Marino's empty office. The day shift had already given way to the night shift when Jack left the station house.

In his old neighborhood, he thought of all the different places he could go for Chinese fast food, but the familiar places now felt empty, unwelcoming, and the lonely winter night finally drove him back to Brooklyn, leaving him staring into a Sunset Park back street of all-night Chinese take-out joints.

Waiting for Buddha

Johnny Wong reached over to a tray in the corner and angled the antenna of the little transistor radio, keeping the Chinese music low-key, a Shirley Kwan Hong Kong pop ballad. He swiveled the antenna until the static cleared, then leaned back on his bunk.

He scanned the dark cement box of a room, closed his eyes when they reached the bars across the front of the cell. He took a deep breath, and again thought about how his life had come to this.

During the first few days of *chor gom,* prison, he'd been mixed in with the *hok gwai,* black devils, and the *loy sung,* the lowlife Spanish. They'd mocked him by pulling back the corners of their eyes, taunting him, *Egg roll! Bruce Lee!! Fock you ass, Jackie Chan! Ching chong!* Some of them menaced him, sizing him up to rob him. A few sadists regarded him as fresh meat, stared him down with hard faces, the way long-term criminals devour new prisoners with their scowling, man-raping eyes.

Johnny had steeled himself mentally; he wouldn't go down easily, would set an example.

Suddenly, he'd gotten transferred to the Central Punitive Segregation Unit, a maximum security single-cell jail. Protective custody. Protective? he'd wondered. From whom? Everyone, he'd realized. Now he was kept from the general population, confined to a six-by-nine-foot cement cage, with a wall bunk across from a metal toilet bowl.

And Shirley Kwan singing.

He remembered purchasing a radio car hookup from the Taxi and Limousine Commission. The overnight limo deal, jockeying the black Lincoln, had prospered, until he made a mistake. He'd broken one of his cardinal rules: *never* get involved with the paying customers

He'd been taken in by her beauty.

Smoldering anger and shame still flared up inside, but he knew it was his own fault. He'd been the greedy fish who'd taken the bait. He'd been socking away cash until he got mixed up with the client, the Fat Uncle's lady, his alluring mistress, Mona. He'd been seduced by the tragedy of her story, her past and her present life of suffering. And, of course, by her sexual beauty, her sensual lovemaking.

The other night drivers had never caught on.

The instant that he entered her, never realizing he'd been sucked in, had led to his present state: imprisoned for a crime he didn't commit. All his grand dreams—a take-out counter, a Wah Wah Bakery franchise, the coin Laundromat deal—gone. All gone. Eventually, he'd have to sell the Lincoln, and move on.

Now his life was in the hands of other men: a Hip Ching tong officer, and a fancy *gwailo,* Caucasian, lawyer. Johnny had gotten over his initial rush of hysteria, had resigned himself to his fate, trusting that the tong agent and the white lawyer would work successfully toward his release.

They'd wanted to find the victim's mistress, the woman known only as Mona. Johnny had helped their Chinese artist draw a likeness of her, a pretty face pulled from the intimate memories he'd had of her. The artist had been forging copies of Rembrandt and Vermeer, and his rendering was far better than a mug shot. Johnny had revealed conversations he'd had with Mona, described her fashion sense, anything that might provide a clue.

Protective custody.

He didn't understand how or why, until he'd met the two men in the interview cell. They had made all the arrangements somehow on the basis of some phone threats against him that had been called into the prison. So they'd had to move him, per regulations.

Now Johnny had a small semblance of the creature comforts of Chinatown. He'd survived these four months in the cinder-block cell because the two men had arranged for him to get twice-weekly rations of *lo mein* and *chow faahn*, fried rice, packs of Marlboros and oolong tea bags, Chinese newspapers and magazines. Most of all, he found comfort in the transistor radio with the special chip embedded that brought broadcasts from Chung Wah Chinese Broadcasting into the prison.

He knew when his care packages of supplies arrived by the smell of fried rice and egg rolls wafting over from the guards' locker room. One of the black guards had given him a packet of extra batteries for the radio, and started calling him "Mister John."

They'd assigned him a half hour each day alone in the exercise yard. He practiced some tai chi exercises, smoked cigarettes, puzzled over where Mona might have gone. He hoped the frigid wind of the yard was somehow touching her also.

After almost four months, Johnny realized that the Hip Chings weren't going to muster up the million-dollar bail bond until they had a handle on the whereabouts of the mistress. Anything that came to mind, he'd let them know. Both men were always encouraging during their visits, insisting that the Hip Chings were determined that "justice be served." With Johnny's help, they'd certainly find her, and in turn, he would be set free.

"It's only a matter of time," the Chinese tong man always said. The way he put things, it was always *when* he'd be released, *when* they'd find the woman, *when* they could help him relocate and start anew.

Dangling hope like a three-section flail, an iron kung fu whip.

He dreaded the feeling that his life was in the hands of these two men. Still, he needed them as much as they needed him, if not more.

A marriage of necessity.

The Caucasian lawyer's part was to manipulate the law during his incarceration. The *tong yen*, Chinese man, managed the Chinese side of things, helping to sublease Johnny's black Lincoln out to the funeral drivers so the car would continue to make money even as he sat in prison.

They'd even paid his monthly rent on the apartment in Brooklyn's Chinatown.

They'd wrapped their control around him like a closed fist.

His emotions came back around to anger. He was mad at himself for falling for Mona's promises, her lies. His bravado, greed, and foolishness had brought him to this cinder-block cell, in this penal colony of *hok gwai* and *loy sung*.

Dew! Fuck! he cursed silently as he remembered how he'd helped her buy a gun off the streets, even loaded it for her. He'd left his prints on the spare clip while she'd sucked him, and suckered him.

Deadly thoughts pulsed inside his head, keeping him awake. Fatigue only brought back images of her glistening naked body against his, her pretty head twisting and bobbing over his groin, until finally black-out sleep swept over him and obliterated the bars of the prison cell.

"Yo, Mister John! Meeting time!"

The guard's bark jerked Johnny into consciousness, brought him to sit up on his bunk, staring into the shiny white teeth grinning at him.

"Yo. Fried rice tomorrow?" the guard said.

Johnny nodded and smiled back, saying "*Tomollo*, okay." He stood, massaging the back of his neck with stiff fingers, trying to press out the tension locked there.

The steel cell gate slid open with a bang and he followed the guard to the interview room. There was a disinfectant smell in the air as they went down the dimly lit corridor.

Law on Order

Johnny's *gwailo,* Caucasian, lawyer, whom he knew as "Lee-mon," wore a charcoal-gray suit and stared at him with blue shark eyes from behind the metallic briefcase he'd opened on the interview table.

Next to him sat brother Tsai Ming Hui, who looked as if he were in his late twenties like Johnny himself, and who, representing the Hip Ching Benevolent Association, was involved in his defense. Ah Tsai's wire-frame eyeglasses and combed-back hair made him out to be a manager or administrator for his tong sponsors. What rank, Johnny could not determine.

They believed in his innocence but needed to find the missing woman.

He'd had no other recourse from his Rikers Island cell.

As always, they'd reassured him that they'd obtain his freedom, and assist him in relocating elsewhere. Like a witness protection program, he imagined.

The lawyer, "Lee-mon," made announcements in *gwailo* English that Johnny couldn't understand.

"I've filed another motion to reduce bail," Sheldon Littman said, glancing at Tsai, "or to get you transferred to the federal lockup on Pearl Street. I feel they're backing off murder one but we're not accepting manslaughter, either."

"We're trying to get you to a better jail, near Chinatown,"

translated Tsai. "Your lawyer feels that the prosecutors don't have a case." Tsai turned away from Littman, saying, "Also, about the bail: the association's member's restaurants proved to be unreliable as collateral. Too many silent partners."

Johnny nodded, disappointed. He'd heard a similar claim during their last meeting.

"We're canvassing the membership," Tsai continued in a confidential tone. "For houses, family homes we can use toward the bond. We'll have to wait and see."

Johnny had also heard this before; different words, same meaning. He noticed Lee-mon observing Tsai *go*, curious about the long translation of his own brief statements.

Tsai turned to Littman, saying in his Hong Kong English, "Don't be concerned. I am keeping his hope alive." He smiled. "It is a *Chinese* thing."

Littman narrowed his eyes at Johnny, cracked a crooked smile. Tsai, turning back to Johnny, continued, "Now, you said you remembered something."

Johnny hesitated.

"Don't worry," Tsai reassured him, "he doesn't understand Cantonese."

Johnny took a breath. "I had a dream," he began. "Maybe it means something".

"Go ahead."

"She had a lot of different jewelry, I remembered, but she always wore a jade charm. Hanging off her wrist. It was white and gray, with *pa kua*, Taoist, designs on it. Round, like a coin, a nickel."

"Was she religious?" asked Tsai.

"I don't think so. But I heard her praying once."

"Praying?"

"Like chanting."

"Buddhist?"

"Maybe. She did it low, almost whispering. And she stopped when she became aware of my presence."

Tsai was silent. Buddhist, he thought, so it would be wise to check Chinatown temples.

Littman interjected, "Tell him what we'll do to the Chinese cop on the stand, once he mentions the missing lady. The person of interest."

Tsai didn't let his annoyance show, but instead smiled quietly at the intrusion.

"Your lawyer," he translated, "assures you the courts will rule in your favor." He nodded at Littman, who seemed pleased.

The Chinese cop, Tsai remembered, the American-born Chinese, the *jook sing*, empty piece of bamboo. They would dredge up his tainted career, his Chinatown misadventures, and destroy his credibility.

"Time's up!" yelled the prison guard, opening the door of the interview room with a bang.

Littman shook Johnny's hand, saying, "No worries, be patient," and watched as Johnny shuffled back toward his cinder-block cell.

Tsai stayed behind Littman and followed the guards out, thinking, Buddhist temples and Chinese jewelry stores.

Back to the Future

The long detail in the Chinatown Precinct had exhausted Jack. He was happy to be back on days in the Ninth, the 0-Nine.

The previous day's reports were loaded up on the computer blotter: A teenage wolf pack of a dozen black and Latino youths had assaulted and robbed a Russian immigrant couple in the Alphabets. They'd smashed the man over the head with a brick, and were attempting to rape the woman when patrol arrived and scattered them. On the outskirts of Chinatown, an Organized Crime Control Bureau detail raided a warehouse and confiscated seventy-five thousand dollars' worth of bootleg and contraband cigarettes. Fake Camels and Marlboros from China. The Ghost Legion was involved somehow, thought Jack. Earlier, a man stabbed another man in a Chinatown nail salon. Ming Chu, twenty-six, knifed another Asian man and was charged with second-degree attempted murder and first-degree assault. The motive was unclear. In the East Village, a crew of thugs robbed a Korean deli, wounding the owner's sister. In NoHo, two illegal Chinese nationals were arrested for making high-end purchases with counterfeit credit cards. The two were caught with sixteen bogus credit cards in their possession.

The three Chinese-involved cases had Prosecutor Bang Sing's name attached to them: he was a Chinese ADA saddling up against Chinese criminals the same way that Jack was pitted against the Chinatown underworld.

The shooting space consisted of eight shallow stalls, each with a small counter that looked out over twenty-five feet toward the target end of the range.

Alex saw a series of paper targets clipped onto cable wire, vibrating to the concussion of multiple volleys and staccato bursts of gunfire. Stepping inside the enclosure, the shooter already had "ears" on, noise-canceling headsets that muffled the continuous explosive gunshots from the stalls, where civilians and professionals blasted away with everything from .22s to .9-millimeters to .45s. A deafening barrage of deadly projectiles.

The smell of cordite and gunshot residue filled the air.

The shooter usually clipped a target to the wire, reeled it out to a desired distance, and donned protective eyewear. Weapons were loaded and reloaded on the small counter-top as shooters settled themselves, preparing to fire away.

Alex leveled the Smith & Wesson Ladysmith, taking a breath as she focused on the large body target ten feet away, a threatening dark silhouette. Using a two-handed stance, with her free hand cupped under her gun fist, she felt the fight of the trigger, and squeezed off a one- and a two-shot burst. Paused. Then two more. *Bam! Bambam! Bambam!* And she still had three shots left in the model 317 Airlite, an eight-shot .22-caliber revolver that Jack had recommended.

It weighed less than ten ounces on an aluminum alloy frame, had a black rubber grip, and a smooth combat trigger. Eight shots from a revolver was a definite advantage, and the piece fit nicely inside her designer handbag. The high-velocity long-rifle bullets could rip a hole through a phonebook and still take out an eye.

Jack had warned her, "You shouldn't be capping anybody more than ten feet away. Otherwise, it ceases to be self-defense. And don't go chasing after them, either, for Crissakes."

Alex chuckled at the memory, put the gun down, and reeled in the target. She ran her index finger over the little holes in the black-paper torso-shaped target: a single hit on the right shoulder, then two more across the breastplate, grouped closer together. The last two only an inch apart, just under the heart.

The way Jack had taught her: Shoot to kill. Or don't shoot at all.

The .22-caliber load, even with the high-velocity rounds, had very little kick and was easy to handle. Alex had developed a relaxed natural style, letting loose a volley from different defensive positions: combat conditions. She even felt she could make a torso hit shooting from the hip.

"Yeah, right," Jack had teased. "A real Annie Oakley."

She looked over her shoulder as gunshots thundered from the stalls around her, saw Jack on the other side of the Plexiglas window. He was smirking and giving her a thumbs-up.

She flashed him a small wave of her hand.

"Freakin' too good," Jack whispered to himself, watching Alex through the big picture window that opened on six of the dark stalls, part of the soundproofed dividing wall that separated the lounge area from the target range. She was wearing a dark outfit—black vest and jeans—which reminded Jack of an avenging angel.

The lounge area consisted of a soda machine, a bathroom, and a long couch where members could sit and wait if the place was fully occupied. There was a stack of gun magazines on a folding table: *Hunting Guide; Sportsman's World; Competition Shooting.*

Alex was beginning to shoot instinctively, Jack knew, becoming one with the little lady's gun that was lightweight but deadly. He knew she could make Swiss cheese out of some punk-ass wilding gang looking to jack some weak Asian woman.

The shooting club was managed by Alvin Lin, a thirtyish ABC—American-born Chinese—who was even more *jook sing*, empty piece of bamboo, than Jack. He was a real Chinese cowboy.

Alex shot eight cycles of the five-shot sets, and finally banged off the extra three rounds into a two-inch grouping just beneath the target's abdomen. She loaded the last four bullets into the Ladysmith, keeping seven shots ready but leaving empty the eighth, the firing pin chamber.

"In case you drop it," Jack had explained, "so it won't go off."

She nestled the gun into its case, locked it. Coming out of the shooting area, she took off her "ears" and eyewear, the revolver cooling in the metal box.

"Got done quick, huh?" teased Jack.

"Yeah, I shot the box," she quipped. "What, you expected me to go to war in there?"

Jack grinned. "No, but I'm glad you got it off your chest."

"Right. And how much GSR is on my arm right now?"

"C'mon," Jack said, laughing. "You're watching way too much *Law and Order*."

They decided to go to the East Village for sushi and sake, but Jack's cell phone trilled the moment they left the gun club. Alex caught Jack's end of the conversation, and knew their plans were about to go awry.

"He asked for me?" questioned Jack, a puzzled look crossing his face.

The Chinatown precinct duty sarge answered, "He said the *Chinese* cop. The one who worked the gang shooting. That would be you."

"That's me," Jack agreed. "I'm on my way."

Alex saw Jack's jaw clenching and said, "Well, I've got an early morning anyway. So . . . rain check, okay?"

"Sure, rain check," Jack answered, his thoughts already pointing his gut downtown.

They caught a cab to Alex's Chinatown high-rise, Confucius Towers. From there it was a two-block walk to the 0-Five, the Fifth Precinct.

The evening was dark, but not as black as Jack's mood.

The white, crewcut, uniformed cop met Jack in the detective's area of the squad room, and turned over a large knife in a sheath. Jack pulled the knife out, impressed by its heft. It was a Taiwanese knockoff, a cross between a Crocodile Dundee and a Bowie blade, several inches short of a machete. A deadly piece of tempered steel.

Jack holstered it and dropped it into a file cabinet, locking it.

"He's in the room," said the uniform. "They grabbed him off Delancey Street. He don't talk English too good."

Jack smirked at the irony of what he was hearing.

Sitting in the interview room was a beefy-looking Chinese kid, maybe twenty-one but he looked younger. On the table was a Boston Red Sox baseball cap.

"Man, I'm glad to see you," the kid said when Jack walked in.

"Okay, so you speak English," challenged Jack. "Why are you pretending?"

"I wasn't! No disrespect. But the white cop was outta line. I didn't want to talk to him the way he was playing me."

"So you spoke to him in *Chinglish*?"

"And I asked for you."

"You know me?" Jack asked bluntly.

"I'm cousin of the Jung twins," said the young man.

Jack narrowed his eyes at him, said, "Yeah, and . . .?"

"You know, they got themselves killed in that shoot-out at Bowery? Near OTB? *Your* case; it was in the papers."

"Go on," pushed Jack.

"The cop pulled me over, near the bridge. Said I didn't signal the lane change, something. He checked my plates. Then he started talking crap about how the Red Sox suck and made me get out of the car. The other cop lifted my jacket off the front seat and saw the knife."

"What the hell are you doing with that?" pressed Jack.

"I work in a warehouse. We use it on the job."

Jack poked his finger at the red ball cap, and said, "Boston, huh? What're you doing down here?"

"I came up for the hundred days."

"Hundred days?"

"Go to the cemetery, you know, pay respects. *My two cousins.* You're Chinese. You know, you *understand.*"

Jack remembered: the Jung twins, victims of the brazen shoot-out between factions of Lucky's Ghosts. The "hundred days" after the burial, when Chinese people visit the deceased, was an ancient tradition.

"Well, they *can* charge you with carrying a concealed weapon," warned Jack.

"What concealed? It was on the front seat. We keep it out to cut ropes and cartons, for deliveries."

"The officer says it was in your jacket."

"No way! I took my jacket off in the car. It was hot and I put it on the seat. It may have been covering the knife but I wouldn't call it *hidden.*"

Jack shook his head disdainfully.

"No, man, no," pleaded the kid. "It wasn't concealed. And I wasn't carrying it."

Jack remained stone-faced. "If they press it, you're looking at a coupla nights in the Tombs. Maybe Rikers."

The Boston Chinese started pumping his knee, nervous, fearful because the Chinese cop wasn't helping him.

"Then you'd need to raise bail," Jack added, "and your Boston shit is going to get screwed by your being busted in New York. At the very least, you'd have a lot of explaining to do back home."

"Look, help me out, huh?" Desperate now.

"Tell me why I should," Jack challenged. "Because we're Chinese?" Raising the ante. "Because what?"

"Because I got something that maybe can help you?"

"Yeah, and what's that?"

"There's someone missing from that shoot-out. A punk-ass named Eddie, right?" There was a hopeful tone in his voice.

"How do you know *that*?" asked Jack, raising an eyebrow.

"He's with the *dailo*'s crew. And no one's seen him since."

Jack was quiet a moment. He'd suspected that Eddie Ng had been one of the shooters, but it was all circumstantial.

"So you know where he is?"

"Something like that."

"Don't *fuck* with me, boy," snapped Jack.

"Help me out?"

"Talk," Jack waited.

"He's from Seattle." The kid's words followed a deep sigh. "My cousin mentioned it last year." Both of his knees were pumping now.

"Where in Seattle?"

"That's all I know. Chinatown, maybe."

"Maybe? There's a lot of Chinese in Seattle, boy."

"That's all I know. Please."

Jack shook his head in disbelief, and left the kid in the room. The uniformed cop gave Jack the kid's driver's license while he sweated it out. Jack took the information and ran it for priors and warrants as he reviewed the OTB shoot-out case file.

The reports had tallied up six dead near OTB; five were confirmed Ghost gangbangers, and the sixth was an old Chinese man who'd happened to be in the wrong place at the wrong time and caught himself a cardiac.

The final victim was the Ghost Legion *dailo* himself, Lucky, who might never regain conciousness.

Seattle PD already had Eddie's juvenile mug shot that Jack had forwarded via the Wanted posters, but if they focused on Eddie's height of four foot seven, they'd have a better chance of spotting him. There were a lot of short Chinese around, but not too many that short.

Jack decided he'd give Seattle PD a reach-out and a heads-up, see if Eddie turned up in the older West Coast Chinatown.

Priors and Warrants came up negative for the Boston Chinese kid. Jack had already figured the arrest was a "meatball" bust anyway, with an overzealous cop trying to make a weapons-possession rap off a questionable traffic stop, a case that'd probably be tossed by a grand jury, more waste of taxpayer money and time.

Jack went back into the room.

The kid's eyes were big, scared, hoping against hope.

"First thing," Jack said. "You can forget about getting the knife back." He flipped the driver's license onto the table and the kid sat straight up. "Second," Jack continued, "Don't come down here again." He tossed him his Red Sox cap. "Next time they'll grab you for 'driving while Chinese.' Know what I'm saying?"

The kid jumped up and practically kowtowed to Jack all the way out the door. Jack heard his footsteps bounding down the stairs to freedom.

Putting away the OTB shoot-out case file, Jack decided to give Billy Bow a call.

Neighborhood Blood

"Yo, Jacky boy." Billy Bow's voice came chuckling out of Jack's cell phone.

"I need your help—" began Jack.

"Like Batman needs Robin. What else is new? *Shoot.*" Billy snickered at his own cleverness.

"How many Ngs are there in Seattle?"

"Is this a trick question?"

"Serious, man," said Jack, grinning.

"You sure you don't want Lees or Wongs? I heard they're on sale this week."

"C'mon. Serious."

"Well, there's gotta be hundreds, right? Maybe thousands."

"Yeah, thanks a lot." Jack sighed.

"Look, I can check with one of the old-timers later, *lo oom.* He belongs to the Eng Association."

"Let me know, Blood," Jack said.

"Bet. Anyway, did you hear the joke about Chinese math?"

"Later, Billy," Jack said abruptly. "Tell me when I see you."

Inside the Tofu King, Billy was ready with his jokes.

"Check out this Chinese math," he began.

"Aw, c'mon," Jack protested.

"Nah, listen."

Jack rolled his eyes, shook his head, and resigned himself.

"If three Chinamen jump ship with six ounces of China White, and then chase the dragon three times each before delivering the remaining heroin to the tong, how far will they get if they flee by rickshaw, going six miles an hour, before the pursuing hatchetmen catch them and chop them into eighteen pieces for dipping into the product?"

"Where do you get this stuff from?" Jack chuckled. "The rickshaw drivers work for the tong, right?"

"Damn right." Billy laughed. "They didn't have a China-man's chance to begin with."

"So what do you have for me?" reproved Jack.

Billy paused for effect. "Two hundred eighty-eight Ngs in Seattle. That's including Engs, *with* the 'E.'"

Jack knew the surname was written and spoken only one way in Chinese. "The old man said that? Two hundred eighty-eight?"

"He said the Seattle Eng Association has about two hundred members." Billy grinned at Jack's confusion. "The Seattle local directories, man," teased Billy. "You can look that shit up on the Internet, you know."

"Didn't know you were a computer nerd," Jack retorted.

"Just surfin', dude. Plus, there's no telling how many Engs floating around illegally, know what I'm saying? Add another coupla hundred."

Jack grimaced at the daunting challenge, a thin lead based on a desperate kid's bid to stay out of Rikers, and nothing had come back on the Wanteds, not from Seattle or anywhere else.

Seattle PD would have been looking for a wanted likeness

based on an old juvie photo. In view of that department's inefficient and racist past, what were the chances they'd look hard for someone who hadn't been charged with any crime?

"Watcha expect?" Billy said. "All Chinamen look alike, right? You think white cops are gonna put a big effort behind this?"

Jack frowned at the cynical truth in Billy's words.

"Shit," Billy continued, "you'd do better going out there yourself. Pull up a squat in the middle of Chinatown and watch it roll by."

"Yeah, right," Jack replied sardonically. "Not a China-man's chance, huh?" He backed out toward the front door, waved, said, "Thanks for the math."

"Don't mention it," said Billy grinning. "And don't let the door slap your ass on the way out."

The bilingual Chinatown directory from Seattle's Chinatown Community Center proved to be very useful. Mona quickly located Ping Wong Beautician Supplies and purchased a medium-length gray wig. The booklet offered listings for local discount stores and thrift shops where she bought a drab sweater, black slacks, and a cheap down jacket, all made in China. She found plastic magnifier eyeglasses, looped on a beaded chain, at a Chinese pharmacy. She wore no makeup, and the clothing and accessories helped her appear more matronly: an aging spinster.

Mona easily blended into the rear of the group of *wah kue*, overseas senior citizens, as they boarded the bus to Vancouver. Avoiding the mentholated scent of *mon gum yao*, tiger balm, she made her way to the back.

She enjoyed the view from the window seat as the Seniors Weekend Junket rolled north out of Seattle's Chinatown through the cold city morning.

The charter bus gained speed once it reached the highway. She noticed the number ninety-nine on many signs, *nine* being a yang number, an auspicious place in the *fung shui*. In the system of I Ching trigrams, nine was the element of gold. She thought about her cache of jewelry, the gold Panda coins she'd hidden.

The city blurred past outside the window as she caressed

a jade charm nestled in her right palm, closing her eyes to find a quiet space.

She was stroking the contours of the arrangements of raised lines and sharp etchings like a rosary, feeling above and below the surface of the jade talisman.

The white jade octagon, a *bot kwa* I Ching talisman, was the size of a fat nickel. It was not Shan or Ming dynasty; it was quality jade but not rare. The charm had been a gift from her mother, her only memento, and had touched three generations of the women of her family. It was her mother's *soul.*

On its flat sides, in bas-relief, were symbols of the Eight Trigrams. *Yin* and *Yang* together representing the eight elements of the universe: heaven, earth, wind, fire, water, thunder, mountain, lake. The center of the charm was carved into two embryonic snakes chasing one another's tails, forming the forever changing symbol of the *Yin Yang*, harmony of the cosmic breath.

Mona had learned to read the symbols, Braille-like, in a single passing of her finger, feeling the lines of the hexagrams. She pondered the prophecies in her mind. Dragging her thumbnail across the etched series of lines, she sought guidance and direction, a prophecy from the *I Ching*, the *Book of Changes.*

The combination of lines and broken lines kept coming back to the hexagrams *Thunder over Wind* and *Heaven over Wind*: the sky roars, the wind howls. All regret is gone. Go forward over the Great Mountain.

She measured her breathing.

Wind over Heaven read the hexagrams: a new career, opportunity—but also, conflict, misfortune. Opening her eyes she saw a darkening sky with heavy clouds promising rain. She felt anxiety in the air, an impending storm.

In the face of violence, one must withdraw.

The vistas changed as they left behind the skyline of high-rises, rolling toward the grim mountains in the far distance. She saw rugged bedrock ridges, steep-walled valleys, pristine wilderness, a lake, and a section of river. They came through rolling uplands, the far-off jagged peaks towering above them. Occasionally, she caught a glimpse of the ocean, beyond a stretch of bays that were dotted with green-brown islands.

The natural vistas reminded her of her journey across America, on a one-way train from New York to *Saam Fansi,* San Francisco. It did not seem that long ago. Now she was hundreds of miles farther north, evidenced by the colder weather and the unrelenting rain. From her next destination, Vancouver, once she moved there, she could head south to Chinese communities in Peru, or east to Toronto or Montreal, or even farther east to Europe, England or France perhaps.

The world of the *wah kue,* overseas Chinese, seemed boundless.

An hour into the tour, she smelled the aroma of *po nai,* tea, *cha siew baos,* roast pork buns, and assorted *dim sum* that the other old women produced from their nylon shoulder bags and plastic thermoses.

But they were finished with breakfast by the time the tour bus crossed into the checkpoint.

An immigration agent came aboard and checked the driver's papers. He looked over the group of elderly Chinese women, and silently took a head count, matching the total against the manifest. He glanced at his watch, looked around cursorily, and stepped off the bus.

The line of vehicles had backed up along the highway, idling well beyond the checkpoint, the air thick with exhaust and the smell of rubber.

The agent waved the charter tour bus through.

No passport needed, Mona noted, an easy pass.

The brief stop had allowed the winter cold aboard. Mona felt the chill and was glad to have worn the cheap down jacket.

Back on the road, she noticed that some of the signs were in French. The highway led them to a bridge over a river, and abruptly to a big city spread below them—steel and glass towers, a modern metropolis set against a backdrop of dark but majestic mountains.

She squeezed the jade, pressed out *Fire over Mountain*. Auspicious for the traveler. There is promise in the journey.

Soon enough they were passing under a huge Chinatown gate in *Won Kor Wah*, Vancouver, tall concrete columns supporting a facade of yellow ceramic dragonheads in a classic pagoda motif. She saw buildings and parks bearing Chinese names, and Chinese words on the street signs.

There were old, narrow buildings, many of which were rundown, showing an older traditional Chinatown. They visited a classical Chinese garden dedicated to Dr. Sun Yatsen, father of modern China.

She purchased a souvenir letter opener from a gift shop. It resembled a dagger and its metal handle was embossed with a colorful dragon design over the word CHINATOWN.

Weighing its heft in her hand reminded Mona of Fa Mulan, the woman warrior.

She put the souvenir dagger into her handbag. Then something red caught her eye; it was a red jade bangle. A simple jadeite bangle that was colored dark red, like chicken blood. Real red jade was rare, and she knew this bangle was only a gift-shop trinket, but she wanted to add to her luck. Red jade was especially lucky, and also brought longevity. It inspired courage.

She purchased it as well, and while slipping it onto her unadorned left wrist, she stepped back into the Vancouver Chinatown afternoon. Walking along the streets she heard Toishanese and Cantonese dialects, and even Spanish. Chinese from Peru, she guessed, from Mexico, perhaps Panama.

The tour guide announced they were scheduled for dinner at the Good Fortune Restaurant.

The bus wound its way through the city. She saw British signs that reminded her of Hong Kong places: Queen Elizabeth Theatre, King George Place, Stanley Park.

They passed through a Japantown. The Japanese maple and cherry trees were pretty, she thought, but the history of hatred made her feel sad.

The dinner at Good Fortune was very tasty, but inferior to the Chinese feasts she'd attended in New York. Gone now, she remembered, for good.

Afterward, the old women checked into their rooms at the Budget Inn, where the Chinese staff made everyone feel at home. They were expecting an eventful day tomorrow so most of the seniors retired early.

On the second day, the tour bus brought them to a different part of the city, to a different Chinatown where the buildings were new and tall, where the streets were clean, and the Chinese signs barely noticeable.

The community didn't look like a Chinatown, more like the modern Golden Village that it was called. The seniors enjoyed lunch at one of the many fine restaurants inside a huge luxury shopping mall. Most of the businesses were Chinese-owned, and the shoppers appeared more affluent, stylish, and exuded a fresh young energy.

Mona imagined that she could start anew here.

The tour group was allowed to roam the streets for an hour. Mona purchased two daily newspapers, *Ming Pao* and *Sing Tao*, to read on the trip back, thinking about local news and listings. She bought a Chinatown tourist map from a newsstand, and tried to memorize the streets as she walked, taking business cards from tea shops, clothing stores, Chinese supermarkets, and banks. New destinations, she thought.

She overheard conversations in mainland-inflected Mandarin and Taiwanese.

There was an international airport nearby.

The afternoon turned to evening as they returned to the older Chinatown, to a buffet dinner at a banquet-style restaurant. The Budget Inn was within walking distance, and she finished the night going over the Chinese newspapers and watching the Chinese-language satellite TV news.

It began to snow the next morning, and after a *dim sum* breakfast they returned south along the Interstate. The sky had turned to slate as Mona gently fingered the charm.

Earth over Thunder, it sang. Return. No troubles at home. All is well.

She took a deep breath. Welcome help. Time is on your side.

She was keeping faith, in the *yin* and *yang*.

In the balance of the universe.

Fan and Sandal

He watched the stick of incense burn down beside the figurine of Kwan Kung, God of War.

"We'll see how clever the little whore is," said Gee Sin, the *bok ji sin*, White Paper Fan, sipping at his tumbler of XO cognac. He huffed into the cell phone to Tsai, the *cho hai*, Grass Sandal, his liaison at the other end of the long-distance line.

Outside the high-rise picture windows, the Hong Kong night covered the panoramic sweep of Victoria Harbour, its neon lights and colors dancing off the dark water toward the Tsim Sha Tsui waterfront. Stretching out on the Kowloon side were the city lights of Yau Ma Tei and Mongkok, sparkling in the distance like a scattering of diamonds. A full moon was overhead.

Down to his right, to the mean streets of Wan Chai, and then sweeping all around, was the power and money of the waterfront districts.

Gee Sin was pleased with the information. Chinese jewelry stores. After all, she couldn't *eat* the one-ounce gold Panda coins she'd stolen from Uncle Four, or the fistfuls of diamonds. She'd have to sell or trade them at some point. Then the underground money traders would expose her.

He resolved to be patient, studying his reflection in the mirror wall of the Mid-Levels condominium: a bald pate with bushy brows flecked with gray, oversaggy eyes. An old face. At sixty-three years of age, he was the triad's number three in command, holding a 415 rank, which was a magic Chinese number. Only the *hung kwun*, enforcer, and the *Shan Chu, Lung Tau*, the Red Circle Dragon Head himself, were above him.

The *Hung Huen*, Red Circle Triad, had devolved from their long past nationalism and noble resolve to overthrow the corrupt Ching dynasty, and to restore the Ming era. Patriotic honor had given way, in a matter of decades, to the greed, power, and bloodlust of the modern world. The Red Circle had more than a hundred thousand members, half of them in Hong Kong and China, the others operating in overseas Chinatowns scattered across the globe. This triad organization was only one of dozens of powerful secret societies that controlled the world's heroin trade and a cycle of dirty money, billions of dollars feeding into and out of gambling, prostitution, stock manipulation, and financial fraud that crossed the oceans and touched every continent.

In the near corner stood a life-sized terra-cotta Chinese warrior, a dusty veneer covering his armor, the sword in his hand. One of the many from the thousands of clay warriors taken from Sian by the Red Circle.

Guarding the emperor.

Guarding Paper Fan.

He remembered the first of the Thirty-six Strategies of the society: *Cross the ocean without letting the sky know.* He was lost in memories of his initiation until more information came over the phone.

"Her mother may have been Buddhist," Tsai, the *cho hai*, continued. "She died long ago."

Yet another direction to follow, thought Gee Sin, but well worth consideration. "Have the members check the temples," he advised, "but do not add more people to the search. Keep to the chosen few, your discreet men. Women are even better. The monks are clever and will see through lies. But Buddha is merciful, compassionate. Tell your comrades to plead with the monks; convince them that Mona is a beloved relative who has been diagnosed with cancer. Say that she is afraid but if she doesn't get treatment she will surely die. Your sandal ranks need to be extremely diligent. When we find her, everyone will be well compensated."

Gee Sin didn't want to use the 49s, the *say gow jai*, the dog soldiers. They'd surely muck things up, spook the prey. They were good enough as street muscle, but lacked the sophistication to carry out a quiet search for the whore. Paper Fan had dispatched only the Grass Sandal ranks to conduct the search and pursuit. She can run, he mused, but she cannot hide forever.

"It is simply a function of time," he said to Tsai. He didn't think she was still in *Mei Kwok*, the United States, but Chinese communities in the various far-flung cities of the world were connected through the secret societies, and she'd surface sooner or later.

It was almost the period of *Yuen Siu*, the Lantern Festival, and soon the lanterns would be hung up at Wong Tai Sin Temple and a thousand lesser temples worldwide.

The cadre of Red Circle hunters would surely find her then.

He took another sip of the cognac, feeling safe in the luxury of his condo refuge, his fortress and lair, advising Grass Sandal over the secure digital cell-phone connection. He knew it was mid-morning in Tsai's location in New York City and took pleasure in knowing that all the Red Circle's investments in Manhattan properties had been successful, and prices of their real estate remained steady. He commended Tsai before terminating the call.

He poured more cognac and let his mind drift to the society's successes. The Circle had refined forgery, fraudulent credit, and identity theft into an art *and* a science. He reflected again on the Thirty-six Strategies and how he'd added a twist to Number Seven: Create something out of nothing, to use false information effectively. The Grass Sandals were creating false identities, welding real account numbers to paper names, breeding phantoms who would bring millions to the Red Circle.

To steal the dragon and replace it with the phoenix meant stealing account numbers and matching them with new faces. They'd manufactured bogus driver's licenses for picture identification. The fake licenses were computer-generated and virtually indistinguishable from the real deal. Any of the mobile mills, with portable laptops and rented laser printers, could turn out acceptable forged passports and visas as well.

He took another swallow from his glass of cognac, caught his breath, and closed his eyes. He had learned quickly from past operations in Canada. Instead of selling the cards to amateurs who would get caught and call attention to their operation, he'd decided to use selected Chinese people in order to impose control and improve communication. The idea of using storage locations and closed warehouses was his way of adding mobility and volume for the operators. They would fence the scam's products through the triad's legitimate businesses.

Gee Sin, the senior adviser, had taken advantage of the Americans' holiday preoccupation with gift-giving, the annual buying frenzy that overwhelmed what was originally a religious holiday. Paper Fan had quickly realized how important these several weeks were to merchants hoping to rake in sales, which, in the crazed crush of business, made them careless and blind to credit-card fraud.

They'd focused on high-end electronics that the Red Circle could sell easily through its network of merchants, expensive items like video camcorders, digital cameras, and laptop computers. Diamond jewelry and expensive watches. They'd expected to steal tens of millions of dollars' worth of merchandise over the holidays. The legitimate cardholder and the card-issuing company wouldn't detect anything amiss until weeks after the holidays, when the monthly statements arrived in the mail. By then, Paper Fan and his operatives would be long gone, leaving only a trail of smoke and shadows.

His thoughts changed again as he felt a slow throbbing at his left wrist. Occasionally, he'd feel sharp pain there, but this occurred mostly in cold climates like Vancouver or Toronto.

Time to take it off, he thought.

The psychiatric member of the rehabilitation and physical therapy team at Kowloon had suggested to him the idea of residual pain, the severed nerves remembering the moment of the chop. "It's all in the brain," she'd said. "You think you feel pain so you do feel pain." Mostly it was chafing, or too much pressure at the new joint, where scar-sealed bone and muscle bumped against the silicone-padded socket of the prosthesis.

He could remove the prosthesis to relieve the discomfort. Painkiller medication was prescribed if necessary.

Dew keuih, fuck, he cursed quietly. He knew it wasn't the hand. After all, it fit well and he'd trained with it, had *willed* it to work well. It wasn't the hand.

It was the attack that he remembered, hazy now but still horrific even after twenty-five years; the pain of a young man revived in the stump arm of an old man. The glint of light from his left. Raising his *bow arm* reflexively. It wasn't the hand, marvelously sculpted and engineered. He'd been knocked down. When he braced to get up, he saw that he had no left hand. It was the memory.

And he had survived the attack. The chop had been intended for his neck.

Gee Sin detached the elastic and Velcro band that wrapped around his elbow and slipped the hand off. He imagined it as a weapon, nestled in the sling, its holster. He set it down on the black glass coffee table.

The throbbing in the stump ebbed.

Touch

Already five years old, the bionic hand was an ultralite model, a myoelectric prosthesis with articulate fingers, an opposable thumb, a rotating wrist. It was powered by batteries inside the fake limb. Sensors there detected when the arm muscles contracted, then converted the body's electrical signal into electric power. This engaged the motor controlling the hand and wrist, its skeletal frame made of thermoplastics and titanium for extreme flexibility. The frame was covered by a skin of silicone that was resistant to heat and flame, and custom-colored with pigmentation to match the patient's skin. The hand and fingers were sculpted with fingernails, knuckles, and creases. At a glance, it was indistinguishable from a real hand. The hand cost eighty thousand dollars in Hong Kong and the triad had paid without question.

Removing it from his forearm reminded him of the rehabilitation course at the Kowloon Clinic, where he'd trained to use his new artificial limb. He'd continued for a year until his control of hand and finger movements became so deft that he mastered eating with chopsticks and dealing a deck of cards. He could pluck a coin off the table.

He could pull the trigger of a gun.

Aaya, he sighed, finishing off the last of the cognac, letting his thoughts return to matters at hand. He was indifferent to the murder of Uncle Four; the Hip Ching leader had been arrogant and so had brought about his own demise with his whore. His foolishness, however, had cost the Red Circle a cache of gold Pandas and brilliant diamonds, the value of which, though small compared to the billions raked in by combined triad operations, had caused a loss of face. The Hakkanese drug couriers and their Chiu Chao financiers had leaked details of the rip-off.

The Red Circle had lost face, and the whore had to pay.

Death by a myriad of swords was too simple. They'd have to make an example of her, a warning to all others who thought they could steal from the Hung Huen brotherhood. They would videotape a gang rape of her, then pimp her off, *before* killing her, finally making a snuff film for the porno dogs to market, completing the revenge.

The throbbing came back, a slow steady beat. Normally, he'd take a Vicodin and allow it to pass, but tonight he had special pleasures in mind, the kind he didn't want diminished by medication. It was the one thing aging men still clung to. *Desire.* He closed his eyes and pictured the *siu jeer,* "young ladies," who would soon arrive at his condo door, and ignored the pulsing forearm stump.

"Fuhgeddaboudit," Captain Marino said. "There's already a cap on overtime. Unless you have something solid, like extradition, or taking custody and bringing him back, the department's not paying for a fishing trip to the West Coast."

No way. Not on the department's dime.

Jack left the captain's office and exited the Chinatown station house. He turned west on Bayard, following the scent of death and the distant sounds of grief in his head. He walked inside Columbus Park until he came to the rundown asphalt ball fields, the hard-scrabble playground of his Chinatown youth. Across the way, he could see the black cars jockeying for position on the street of funeral parlors.

The other merchants of death were known to be charitable toward the more tragic losses of life. The Chin brothers of Kingdom Caskets would discount the no-frills metal veneer boxes, and Peaceful Florist would charge wholesale for the floral wreaths. The headstone cutter might donate the engraving of the carved Chinese characters. The Family Associations would contribute toward the rest of the funeral expenses. A small group of black-clad mourners burned paper items in a tin bucket, offering up small colorful gifts for the afterlife: a lady's slippers, a man's tie.

Jack smelled the odor of jasmine, incense drifting in the winter air as the black Town Cars and Continentals lined up behind the DeVille flower wagon filled with wreaths of carnations and mums.

The Wah Fook Parlor had six death notices posted on their doors. May Lon Fong's funeral was the next one. Outside the Wah Fook, eight Chinese musicians had assembled, all wearing full-length *min-nop* coats of brown silk with black fedoras, watching the mourners from behind dark sunglasses as they tuned their instruments: four Chinese *suona* horns, two mournful *erhu*, string violins, a bamboo folk drum, and a small harp.

Jack hadn't seen such a large funeral band before. They tuned up to a big symphonic sound as the procession began. Normally, Jack would have attended the wakes, paid his respects, but this murder-suicide was doubly tragic, and he decided to get his closure from a distance.

Farther down the street, Harry Gong's funeral continued behind the closed doors of the Wing Ching Parlor. The families had decided on separate funerals, unable to reconcile the memories of killer and victim. Their hands rigidly clasped together at the end of life, they were now bound for different cemeteries.

The Chinese band began playing their dirge as the pallbearers brought May Lon's casket out, stepping in cadence toward the black Cadillac DeVille with her black-and-white photograph braced atop. A small crowd murmured their sadness in the frozen morning air as her family and relatives followed the casket. Suddenly, a harrowing cry burst from the group as May Lon's mother ran past the pallbearers loading the DeVille and threw herself across the coffin. "Aayaaa!!" she screamed, the veins in her neck standing out as she beat her chest and tore at her hair. Other relatives rushed in, lifting her away from the coffin. She fell to the pavement, kicking, pounding the asphalt with her heels, on the edge of madness in her despair.

May Lon's father stood speechless, ready to collapse.

They carried the mother into the lead Lincoln Town Car as the other funeral drivers pulled up along the curb, loading up the family and gently moving the procession along. The band played louder as the dark DeVille led the way toward Canal Street. The six-car procession then turned left toward the Holland Tunnel, bound for the Chinese cemetery at Sacred Oaks in New Jersey.

Jack took a few deep *shaolin* breaths through his nose, allowing the sadness to ease. Farther down the block, the doors of the Wing Ching swung open. With no band, no mournful dirge, the pallbearers shouldered Harry Gong's casket as three Lincolns and a black minivan pulled up along the street.

The father wore a grim frown, carrying a smoking baton of mustard-colored incense. He narrowed his eyes as he followed the body of his only son, as if searching in a dark distant realm. Everyone loaded in quickly, quietly, eager to bring the deceased to the serenity of his final resting place. The large stick of incense poked out of the window of the first car as the Town Car led the way.

The procession turned east on Bayard, south on Mott, and paused near the Wong Sing Restaurant on Pell, where the day shift bowed their heads, then proceeded to the Bowery, where it held up Lower East Side traffic, pausing for eight seconds at the Nom San Bok Hoy Benevolent Association, before rolling onward.

The black caravan made its way through the icy daylight and took the Williamsburg Bridge on the way to the Chinese section of Heaven's Pavilion Cemetery.

The funerals had cast a pall over Jack's mood and he exited the park to get away from the street of mourning, unsure whether any closure had come for him.

Golden Star

Feeling hungry and thirsty, Jack sat in the last booth in Grampa's, watching the television above the bar while waiting for his order of onion-smothered steak. He took a long pull from his bottle of Heineken and considered jetting out to Seattle for a long weekend, subtracting a few NYPD vacation days. He'd hang out with Alex, there to receive her ORCA award. He could touch base with Seattle PD and check the layout of Seattle's Chinatown and the International District area.

The television displayed a press conference featuring the new Italian-American mayor, who was pitching the idea of banning fireworks in Chinatown, especially Chinese New Year celebrations. The mayor was citing fire safety concerns. It hadn't been a concern for a hundred and twenty-five years, thought Jack, but suddenly, it was a problem. All the Chinese knew that it was the mayor covering his ass after resolving to go after the mob at the Fulton Fish Market, and the Mafia's defiant display of July Fourth fireworks in Brooklyn and Staten Island's Italian enclaves.

With contempt, Jack took another swallow of beer. No *firewoiks* for the *paisans,* no Chinese New Year celebration for the Chinks. Non-Chinese citizens didn't realize the banning of fireworks in Chinatown would allow evil spirits to creep back in, into the Lower East Side and all of New York City as well.

Jack wondered if fireworks would become just a loud smoky memory, as they had in Los Angeles, San Francisco, and other major Chinatowns in America.

He could smell the onions from the kitchen, the aroma pulling at his nose, spiking his appetite. The bar was almost empty except for a couple of suit-and-tie business types in the far booth near the entrance. They reminded Jack of the CADS, Alex's legal friends, the Chinese-American Defense Squad.

Jack wondered if ADA Bang Sing was a member of their little club, if he had a connection to Alex that was other than professional. CADS? He wondered why it mattered. Was he jealous? Or was it just leftover romantic uneasiness from his party dream, the one that had featured Alex, on the night he'd gotten pulled into the murder-suicide?

CADS? They were an activist group, self-starters and true believers, the kind Alex liked to run with, out to wreak havoc on a cumbersome, misguided justice system. One of the judges who was known to lean toward the Radical Left had railed about discriminatory hiring practices and police brutality toward minorities. Jack had heard that two of the lawyers were trust-fund brats, but legal warriors nonetheless. And why did any of it matter to him?

He wondered if Alex's impending divorce was reinforcing her involvement with CADS, as she seemed to bloom when fighting controversial cases.

He remembered Alex at the pistol range. Combat stance. Firing in short bursts. She really was an Annie Oakley, but was she relishing the feel of actually shooting someone, symbolically? In the wake of the cop killing of the Chinese honor student, were her emotions feeding her dead-eye accuracy?

Jack finished his beer, ordered another. You can look that shit up on the Internet, Billy had said when they were talking about Ngs in Seattle. Jack wasn't a cop historian, but he pressed his trigger fingers against his temples, rolling little circles as he closed his eyes, coaxing out what he remembered.

The Seattle Police Department had a checkered past. It had made headline news back in the fifties and sixties, a violent period in the American Northwest. Grand-jury investigative hearings, much like the Knapp Commission hearings in New York City, exposed corruption in the Seattle PD. Abetted by crooked politicians, the Seattle PD's operations included gambling and police payoff scandals. Police took money, turned a blind eye. It was nothing new in the world of cops.

The gambling problem, of course, reared its ugly head in Chinatown, and law-enforcement departments nationwide remembered the 1983 Wah Mee massacre. The Wah Mee had been a Seattle Chinatown gambling and bottle club, one of many, which was allowed to flourish because of the police payola. The Wah Mee had operated high-stakes Chinese gambling games, and on an early February morning a decade earlier, three Chinatown misfits from Hong Kong, desperate and misguided, executed a plan to commit robbery and murder there. The result was thirteen deaths, one survivor, the baring of police payola, and the castigation of the Chinese community by mainstream media. They'd tried to make it seem like it was some sort of tong war incident, *hatchetmen* stuff, rather than the immigrant aberration that it was. All of it reinforced the idea that the police weren't worthy of trust.

Jack continued rolling up the images with his trigger digits, and abruptly, Keung "Eddie" Ng, "Shorty," came to mind. Seattle Chinatown? Jack didn't mind playing long shots, so long as it was convenient to do.

Someone slid softly into the booth, nudging him over, breaking his flow of thoughts.

"Seattle, huh?" Alex grinned. "You're kidding me." She seemed happy about the prospect and ordered a Cosmo.

His steak arrived with the martini, and he cut her a slice. She devoured a piece before chasing it down with the drink.

"It's only a week away," she said. "The Westin's sold out. I'm sharing a double with Joann Lee from Legal Aid because they overbooked."

"No problem," Jack answered, cutting her another slice. "I'm making other arrangements anyway."

"Found a room?" Alex said, raising an eyebrow.

"Soon."

"I hope it's near the Westin," she said over the martini glass. "Most of the events are there."

"No problem," Jack repeated. He didn't want to say he'd be out by the airport, the Sea-Tac Courtyard. Half the price, and a jackrabbit getaway for the return flight. He was going to check out Seattle, not just hang with Alex, and seventy-two hours was not enough time to get it done. Besides, he figured, Alex was going to be plenty busy anyway.

Watching her as she sipped her Cosmo, Jack asked, "What kind of town is Seattle? Does ORCA have issues there?"

Alex set her drink down, answering bluntly, "Do you want to start with glass-ceiling discrimination at Boeing Industries? Or racism at Abercrombie and Fitch? Or do you want to go down memory lane, when they burned down Chinatown and drove the Chinese out of Seattle and Tacoma in 1885?"

"Okay, I get it." Jack chuckled. "A few issues there." He always marveled at how she was able to toss out facts and incidents, like neat little Molotov cocktails, from somewhere not of this time or her own experience. It was if she was speaking for ghosts, giving voice to long-lost souls. "But I meant, more like cop stuff."

"Oh, *that*." Alex lifted her glass, took another sip. "Well, last year Seattle PD was accused of racial profiling. A couple of officers harassed and humiliated an APA youth group who were out on a day trip."

"No shit," Jack said, knowing that APA stood for Asian Pacific American, an expanded and more inclusive identity than *Chinese* or *Other*. He ordered up a plate of clams casino.

"No shit." Alex smirked. "Threw the teenagers up against a wall, screaming insults at them. Held them for an hour. Interrogated them like they were foreign criminals instead of American citizens."

"Were they charged?" Jack asked, disbelief in his tone.

"They were cited for jaywalking."

"*Jaywalking?*" Jack snapped, rolling his eyes. "You mean 'crossing while Chinese'?"

Alex, with a sardonic grin, ordered another Cosmo, lit up a cigarette. "So," she concluded through smoky exhalation, words dripping sarcasm, "other than those minor drawbacks, it's a top-ten city of a destination. High-tech jobs, great schools, excellent outdoors, wonderful place to raise a family, etcetera etcetera." She took another puff of the cigarette. "Lots of rain, though."

Rain, thought Jack, remembering Ah Por's words, her clues. Had she whispered "rain" to Eddie Ng's juvenile photo? Or to the Hong Kong magazine likeness of Mona?

Alex's second Cosmo arrived with the clams casino as Jack shared the last of his steak with her.

"I've got two award ceremonies to attend, one panel discussion, a silent auction, two cocktail parties. And the grand gala dinner-dance for one thousand."

"Can I crash?" teased Jack.

"I've got connections," she mock-boasted. "I can get you in. But you sound like you're going to be busy."

"So do you," he said quietly. "But we'll work it out."

Alex knew better than to probe cop stuff, knew Jack would just talk his way around things, being professional. A real cop's cop, but with an old-timer's sense of honor. Jack was a Chinese-American anachronism, but she liked him because he had a good heart. And he was brutally honest.

They'd become drinking buddies. Friends. And that was where things stood.

They toasted, then went after the clams casino.

Outside Grampa's, the cold night air braced them. The chill was invigorating during the short walk to her condo at Confucius Towers. She held on to Jack's arm, the bulk and weight of him steadying her. She was light-headed after two cocktails.

"You know," she said, "I don't *have to* attend *all* the events."

Jack smiled, but said nothing; he didn't want to make promises he couldn't keep if he picked up a lead.

The wind gusted, and he pulled her closer as they walked.

"I feel like a hot cup of Colombian brew." Alex shivered. "I have this coffee machine, Italian. You feel like having a wake-me-up with sambuca?"

Jack wanted to say yes but was thinking about Lucky, about the lateness of the hour, and the walking distance to Downtown Medical Hospital. And then the trek back to Brooklyn. All that stacked against a beautiful woman and a cup of coffee that probably wouldn't lead anywhere except to disappointment and misunderstanding.

"I'd like that," he said finally, "but there's something I need to check out that can't wait."

"Cop stuff, huh?" Alex sighed, shaking her head.

"Yeah, but how about a rain check?" suggested Jack.

"*Again?*" she teased. "Maybe those checks will pan out in Seattle, ha? *Rain*, right? And they're known for coffee."

"Yeah, right as *rain*," Jack heard himself saying as they entered the Towers complex.

They exchanged hugs and Alex walked past the doorman in the lobby. He watched her as she waited by the elevators, tossing a smile his way. He watched until the elevator swallowed her up.

Jack could see the bright lights of City Hall, not too far from Downtown Medical. He thought about Tat "Lucky" Louie, hooked up to continuing life support. As he quick-stepped his way through the frozen half-mile of night, he wondered how it had all come to this. He knew Eddie Ng, the *malo* monkey, could answer some of those questions.

Downtown Medical was quiet this time of night, already past visiting hours, but the nurse let Jack have his time with Lucky. It wasn't like the patient was going anywhere. The room was monitored and she'd seen Jack the previous times he'd visited.

He stared at Lucky's gaunt, ashen face, noticed the disinfectant smell of decay, death waiting at the door; a deteriorating body connected to adhesive electrodes measuring its heartbeats.

Jack remembered racing across Chinatown rooftops with Lucky, two *hingdaai,* blood brothers, leaping the gaps between buildings. There were three of them then, three teenage pals, before Wing Lee was knifed to death that seventeenth summer of their Chinatown lives.

Jack wasn't sure why he was in the hospital room, watching Lucky's passing moments. He wasn't expecting Lucky to suddenly wake up and give him all the information he needed to close the case, but he felt that being in Lucky's presence was somehow going to provide another clue as to what had happened leading up to the shoot-out at Chatham Square. A clue to how the Chinatown troubles had brought all these cases of death across his desk. Jack hoped, in a farfetched Ah Por-the-seer kind of way, that something would come to him here: a jarred memory, a symbol, a number or an address, *something.* He remembered the serene setting of the Doyers Street back-alley crime scene, where an old man, *ah bok,* had died of a heart attack, slumped up against a wall, and where a young gangbanger lay face-down dead, reaching out his gun hand in the bloody snow, four high-velocity .22s through his back.

Was Lucky involved?

The blazing shoot-out near OTB on Chatham Square was something Jack could understand: a sudden gun battle, instinctive, spontaneous. *Jing deng*, meant to be. But the back-alley killing behind OTB seemed removed, not just physically, from the rest of the bloodshed. What did the old man witness before he'd suffered the heart attack?

Had it involved Lucky?

Jack knew Lucky had had an apartment somewhere in Chinatown, probably paid for by the On Yee. He'd probably also had several crash pads around the neighborhood. Nothing would be under his name, of course, so they would be impossible to trace. Only the gangboys would know all the locations. The On Yee had probably swept through all of Lucky's places already, Jack figured. All the places they *knew* about, anyway. Lucky had had other hiding places, Jack remembered, tenement niches scattered across the rooftops of their childhood.

The life-support machine continued to pump rhythmically as he leaned in toward Lucky's face. In a whisper, he repeated what they used to say as teenagers, "Us against the world, kid."

Jack stepped back, trying for a moment of clarity. Here was his old friend at the far edge of a life in the shadows, a nonentity, nothing in his name, no history. A ghost ironically, the latest *dailo* of the Ghost Legion. Jack remembered how Tat had claimed payback against the punk hotheads who'd killed Wing. Then he'd disappeared into gangdom, born again with the nickname "Lucky," just as Jack was getting his discharge from army Airborne. Their lives went in opposite directions after that.

At 11 PM Jack called for a *see gay,* Chinatown radio car, to take him back to Sunset Park. He closed the curtain to Lucky's space and said good-night to the overnight nurse.

The *see gay* took him back to Brooklyn, to an all-night Chiu Chao soup shack on Eighth Avenue, where he quietly polished off a *siew-yeh,* a nightcap of beef noodles and tripe. Back at home, he felt exhausted but spent the night at his window, waiting for the light of dawn to break, watching the shades of blackness fade to a new morning.

When Mona first arrived in Seattle, she had scoured the listings in the *Wah bo,* overseas Chinese newspapers, settling for a basement rental from a Chinese couple in a two-family house that was formerly Filipino-owned, and was within walking distance of Chinatown.

Concerned about safety, the elderly pair had specified that they'd wanted a female tenant only.

Jing deng, Mona thought. Destiny.

She had told them that her name was Mona, a name she had taken after the Mong-Ha Fortress in Macau, where she'd gone on a gambling junket long ago. She'd paid two months in advance without question, two thousand, *cash.* No paperwork requested or offered.

They were delighted when she said she'd hoped to stay the entire year.

They'd dedicated a slot on the mailbox for her name. There were Filipinos in the neighborhood but she didn't encounter any other Chinese in the area, which suited her just fine. Less chance of acquiring nosy neighbors.

The street sign at the corner read JAMES STREET, the English spelling of which she'd remembered from growing up poor in British Hong Kong, near King James Road.

Thirteen blocks west brought her to the cloudy bay. She passed through a tourist area of restaurants and quaint shops, until the waterfront opened to tracks and piers, a juncture for trains and ferries, ships and buses heading north, or south. Seven blocks south brought her to Chinatown, where she could blend in even as she purchased essential daily items and groceries, and memorized the locations of businesses, post offices, and banks.

Bo bo lay, she thought, step by step. Proceed with caution.

She'd learn the destinations of trains and ships soon enough.

The basement apartment was a large studio room that included a tiny shower and toilet. There was a closet and a wall shelf that served as a makeshift kitchenette, fitted with an electric hot plate, a rice cooker, and a toaster oven, all left behind by the former tenant, a *pinoy* seaman who'd skipped out on the rent. The old couple had recommended a Chinese locksmith, who'd changed the existing cylinder. Mona had purchased new sheets and blankets for the full-size bed that came with the apartment. In Chinatown, she'd found ingredients for quick-fix meals, and had the Oriental Market deliver a hundred-pound sack of rice. It was more than she needed but would serve other purposes.

Her bed faced the door, in proper *fung shui* arrangement. Seated at the foot, she sprinkled some ginseng into the *Ti-Kuan Yin*, Iron Goddess, before sipping from the steaming cup of tea. Scanning the room she saw the small Buddha kitchen god, a mini orange tree and a potted jade plant, a statuette of the Goddess of Mercy, and various *bot gwa,* I Ching charms, facing northeast and fending off evil.

The apartment door was covered in red, the Chinese color of luck, like her new jade bangle, not expensive but lucky. The door was festooned with leftover Chinese New Year decorations she'd scooped up in Chinatown, crimson banners and gold posters proclaiming *chut yup ping on,* "exit and enter in peace," and welcoming long life and prosperity. At the center of this red collage was a big fold-out lucky calendar from Kau Kau Restaurant, from which she frequently ordered takeout. Whenever she approached the door to leave the apartment, she believed she was heading into good fortune.

She'd found a Chinese hair salon seven blocks to the southeast, a left at *Wong Dai gaai,* King Street, another English spelling she'd remembered from King James Road. She'd also learned to avoid certain areas near Chinatown where *gwailo,* white devils, *joy mao,* alcoholics and addicts, aggressively panhandled. A couple had followed her for blocks through the dilapidated neighborhood of men's missions and homeless shelters. She'd heard murmured growls of "China doll" and "Suzie Wong" as they wagged their slimy tongues obscenely at her. She didn't understand the words but felt their angry sexual intent. Men were dogs, she'd remembered from Hong Kong, and these were strays and mutts.

Wong Dai gaai was the way to and from Chinatown, she'd decided, past the small park where elderly Chinese folks in their quilted jackets congregated, played chess, and gossiped away the time.

In Chinatown, the young man at the *Wah chok wui,* Chinese "service center," had reminded her of Johnny Wong. He had been too eager to assist her, overly inquisitive.

Fifty dollars to fill out the immigration forms.

She wasn't looking to get a green card or Medicare.

Mona realized that she still had this effect on men, her beauty apparent even without makeup. The young clerk had spooked her, and she'd left the agency abruptly, but not before she'd discovered that she'd need a social security card, and non-driver's license.

Other identification, like a passport, would follow from there.

She'd needed secrecy because, deep in her heart, she feared dead Uncle Four's thugs would seek her out.

But soon her transformation would be complete.

She'd dumped the Manolo Blahniks and Jimmy Choos in New York, had left behind the Gucci and Chanel outfits, the thousand-dollar designer handbags, the Valentino Sunglass Collectione, the Dolce & Gabbana accessories: all gone.

The fancy restaurants, the racetracks, all the hideaway clubs in New York, in Chinatowns along the East Coast. All gone. Those were perks that had masked her punishment, she'd realized, seeing it now with vision she hadn't possessed earlier; the abuse she'd suffered had led to freedom.

If I allow it to happen, she'd thought, then I deserve it . . .

Because all bad things must end.

As all good things must also end.

The balance of *yin* and *yang*, the way of the universe.

Changing one's habits was like changing one's appearance. No more designer-label lifestyle, she'd thought, they'd be looking for that. Obviously, avoid the nightlife. The night being *their* time, *their* underworld.

If they find me, she resolved, it will be in daylight. *Bok bok gwong gwong*. All clear to see.

And I will not go quietly.

She remembered the letter-opener dagger in her jacket. Be prepared.

The bleak morning brought Jack back to the Ninth, where his vacation days were approved, where he accessed the precinct's computer setup. He tapped into Seattle's Bureau of Vital Statistics but didn't find a birth certificate for Edward Ng. Or for Edward Eng. To Jack, this merely confirmed that Eddie hadn't been born there but may have been relocated there as an infant.

There were twelve Edward Ngs listed on the school-system database but the ages were all wrong. None of them was in his mid-twenties now. Foreign immigrants and their immigrant offspring. Their addresses were spread across the span of the city.

Four of the Edwards had driver's licenses but their DMV photos showed they were older men, and all were over five foot six. Too tall.

The Social Security databank yielded 148 Edward Ngs and Engs across the nation's Chinese communities. All information requests had to be made in person.

Jack took a deep *shaolin* breath, then another, exhaling stress.

He tapped SEATTLE CHINATOWN into the keyboard.

The designation INTERNATIONAL DISTRICT appeared but took a long time to boot up. Jack rubbed his trigger fingers into his temples until the information came up. Compared to New York, Seattle was a small city, a couple of million people spread out across the great Northwest expanse. Chinatown was part of the International District, the I.D., a designation that Chinatown leaders didn't like, seeing it as an infringement of Chinese culture and history there.

The Chinese had arrived in Seattle first, as miners and railroad coolies on the Northern Pacific, but then were driven out by racist hate. *American* hate. They'd created *two* bustling Chinatowns before fleeing to the East Coast, starting over in New York, Boston, Philadelphia, Washington, and Chicago.

The Japanese followed as America turned against the Chinese, becoming the dominant minority group after Congress passed the Chinese Exclusion Acts. They created Japantown. *Nihonmachi.* J-town thrived until World War II happened and America rounded up Japanese-Americans, forcing them into the internment camps.

The Filipinos, who were U.S. allies, founded Filipinotown.

The Vietnamese arrived after the lost war and cultivated the Little Saigon area.

Koreans and Indians added to the international Asian identity.

There were more than twelve thousand Chinese in Seattle, so it wasn't going to be easy the way Billy Bow had joked, like "just pull up a chair" and wait for Eddie to walk by. But who knows? thought Jack. Shit happens.

Altogether, Seattle Asians totaled maybe fifty thousand people, crammed together in a district that mixed and muted all their cultures and true colors. More diversity, Jack realized, but less unity.

New York City, Jack knew, had more than fifty thousand residents in any one of its three Chinatowns. He pushed back from the computer and closed his eyes.

Alex came to mind and he pictured her on a plane somewhere over the Midwest. The CADS and the New York ORCA members, having booked their flights weeks in advance, had arranged for an early departure that would put them in Seattle around noon.

Jack was only able to get a last-minute flight that wasn't scheduled to depart JFK until mid-afternoon. He envisioned early-evening traffic congestion, and rainy skies at Sea-Tac International.

Jack hopped a downtown M103 bus to Chinatown. He didn't see Captain Marino in the 0-Five, but proceeded to make copies of data from his open-case files, reviewing the information as it piled up. He pocketed one of the .22-caliber slugs that had been placed into the evidence file.

It was already afternoon when he caught the *sai ba*, minibus, on Market Street, its harried driver bouncing his passengers toward the Williamsburg Bridge, back to Sunset Park.

In his studio apartment, Jack changed into a black suit, over which he'd planned to wear an all-weather jacket. He tossed a permanent-press shirt and another dark suit into a backpack. He checked his Colt Special, and his badge. The kitchen garbage bag went into the hallway chute.

He made sure his studio's windows were secured, locked, with the shades drawn. It wasn't that he was planning a long trip but in Brooklyn, New York, it was better to be paranoid than sorry.

Knowing that the Chinese drivers were experts at skirting the traffic bottlenecks en route to JFK, he called one of the *see gay* radio cars from Eighth Avenue.

The flight was delayed.

Jack purchased a plastic disposable camera, and tried to work up a profile of Eddie while he waited. Eddie Ng, the *ma lo*, monkey; *bad monkey*. Shorty, the Red Star gang member as a juvenile, breaking-and-entering raps, the tattoos. What part had he played in the Ghosts shoot-out? What was the beef between him and the gang vic in Doyers alley, Koo Jai, a.k.a. Kid Koo?

Seattle was known for its great outdoors activities but Jack didn't feel that Chinatown-wise Eddie was a sailing, kayaking, biking, and hiking kind of guy, especially in the raw weather patterns of the Northwest. Indoors, figured Jack, but probably not bowling, movies, anything like that. He'd want to go somewhere he could blend in, or be left alone. Something solitary. He didn't figure to stray too far from Chinatown, risk losing his *invisibility*.

He found a seat near the boarding gate and fought the urge to close his eyes and catch an hour's worth of power nap.

Curious George the monkey came to mind. . . .

Watching the eight ball, near the side pocket, he knew it was an easy shot. He saw the nine ball next, at the other end of the table, almost against the short rail, two feet from either corner pocket. He casually blew blue chalk off the tip of the stick, put English on the cue-ball stroke, and pocketed the eight. He hadn't put enough draw behind the spin, however. Shit, he cursed quietly.

He'd played it wrong and the white cue ball rolled to the middle of the table, leaving him a long stretch and a hard angle cut-shot to the corners. He'd have to slice the nine ball razor thin and then hope it didn't graze too much rail and bounce.

He chalked up the stick again, scanning the run-down Filipino community center. Most of the kids had gone and it was quiet.

On his tiptoes he leaned full-length across the table and stroked the shot carefully, focused on the slice. He finally flicked his wrist and the white cue ball nipped the edge of the yellow nine, sending it along the rail into the corner pocket, the ball plopping into the worn leather netting that hung beneath the table.

Fuck yeah! he grinned, *dew chut!* Willie fuckin' Mosconi.

He took a breath, saw the dark afternoon outside the center's windows, snow threatened in the forecast. His grin turned into a frown as he checked his watch, considering playing one last rack of balls before calling his *amigos*.

Night Games

The sky was roiling darkness when Jack landed at Sea-Tac at almost 6 PM.

He took an airport shuttle to the Courtyard and checked in. Seattle television news filled the lobby bar, live coverage of a double shooting in the Madrona Park district. Such shootings were routine in New York, thought Jack.

One of the victims was believed to be a city councilman's son. There was a sense of urgency in the administration's tone, and police officials looked grim.

His motel room was small and Jack was glad he had traveled light. He remembered that Alex had a series of workshops scheduled, then a dinner party. He tried calling her room via the front desk but there was no answer.

He washed his face and executed a few *shaolin* stretching exercises to take the stiffness from the long airplane ride out of his joints.

The concierge ordered up a car that took him to Seattle Police Headquarters in the West Precinct, which included Chinatown and the I.D., the International District.

Cops

Jack presented his NYPD identification and detective's gold shield to the cop at the desk. They perused one another's badges momentarily. Jack noticed the Seattle badge had a spread eagle perched on top of the shield with a star in the middle. Not as round as Jack's badge, more pointed.

The young cop at the duty desk had a fresh face and wore a light blue regulation uniform and had a military haircut. The three hash marks on his shirtsleeve meant he had at least three years on the job.

"I'm looking for a person of interest," explained Jack.

"The detectives are out right now," the duty cop replied, snapping shut Jack's badge wallet and handing it back.

"I'm reaching out to them any way I can. I'm only here in Seattle over the weekend."

A moment of sympathy crossed the young cop's face, after which he replied, "All the detectives are out chasing a red ball. They're after POIs, too, but there's *fresh* blood here."

"You're referring to Madrona Park?" Jack asked, knowing that "red ball" meant an all-out manic manhunt for perps.

"Correct," the cop replied hesitantly, surprised at Jack's knowledge. "But you can leave a voice mail. Or a note. Or you can wait if you like." He gestured toward a wooden bench.

No time to wait, thought Jack, offering his PBA card. "I'd appreciate if someone could call me. *Anytime.*"

"No disrespect," the young cop offered, "but honestly, I don't know when any of the detectives will be back. This could go on all night, maybe all tomorrow."

"Thanks," Jack said. "I'm staying at the airport motel, the Courtyard."

"Ten-four," the cop acknowledged. Jack wondered if he'd ever seen a Chinese cop before.

Jack left headquarters and walked through the misting night. Figuring that Alex would be at her dinner deal, he decided to call her later. Chinatown was nearby and he headed in that direction. He knew he couldn't cover all the Chinese restaurants in Seattle, but he wanted to check out the locals, maybe have dinner in one of them.

Walking the small grid of streets, he realized that the names of the restaurants were just like those in New York and in other Chinatowns he'd visited: Canton House; Golden Phoenix; China Dragon; Hong Kong Harbor; May Lay Satay; Hunan Palace; King Mandarin; Kau Kau.

He decided not to flash his badge; he didn't want to scare up local talk that could warn or spook Eddie. In his quiet Cantonese, he informed the waiter that he was awaiting a party of two, and asked if he could use the washroom.

"Of course," answered the waiter, pointing the way. To and from the washroom, Jack was able view the kitchen help, peeping at them in case one was a Chinese shorty. Jack repeated this in six different restaurants, finding nothing, before he felt hungry enough to have dinner. It was already after 8 PM when he chose May Lay Satay, ordering Singapore rice noodles with a side of *roti canai*, keeping his eyes on the kitchen area.

Maybe Patrol would pick up something down the line, he thought, after the red ball.

The food was good but he didn't see anyone remotely resembling Little Eddie.

He remembered that he needed a map and the White Pages, so he requested them from the Courtyard concierge. It was after 9 PM and he called Alex in her hotel room.

"Hey," she said, fatigue edging her voice.

"Done already?" Jack asked.

"They went drinking," she said, annoyed. "Macho stuff, when we have an early morning tomorrow. I'm presenting at the youth awards breakfast."

"Don't feel like drinking?" teased Jack.

"I had drinks at dinner." Alex yawned. "And I've been up since dawn."

He'd thought she'd be ready for a nightcap but said, "Okay, I get it. You're *beat*."

"Right, I'm tired and I don't need to go drinking."

He wasn't sure if she was referring to the CADS or dropping him a hint.

"You're right," he said, "Get some rest. Tomorrow's another day."

"I'm free around mid-afternoon," she offered, some cheer in her voice. "We can make up for that rain check, maybe."

Mid-afternoon, thought Jack, replying, "Sure, let's see what happens." Play it by ear.

"Okay then, call me," she said. "Or leave me a message."

"Sure thing, ten-four," he kidded. "And good night." He heard the *click* at her end as she hung up.

Jack considered snooping at a few more restaurants but

it was already nine thirty, and the dinner crowd would be a wrap. He peered into the alleys of the restaurants he passed along the way, watching out for any short *da jop*, kitchen help, bringing out the black plastic bags of restaurant garbage.

He'd have to get back to his room, a half-hour ride to the motel. He purchased a tour map at a Jackson Street gift shop, noting the areas around the International District, assessing the ground he'd have to cover in the sixty hours he had left.

After Jack got back to the Courtyard, the concierge sent up a White Pages and a general street map of the city as requested. Plotting out his strategy, Jack knew he'd have to get an early start. It would be a busy Saturday morning and he had a hunch he wanted to follow up on.

But what if his hunch was all wrong? Eddie *would* have to find work but if he was an American-born Chinese, ABC, or *jook sing*, then he wouldn't be limited to Chinese-language-only businesses.

Maybe he didn't need to work and was just hanging out, enjoying his freedom. But where would he hang out?

Jack considered Chinese videotape shops where Eddie might rent kung fu movies, or porno flicks. He wondered if Eddie visited Asian massage parlors. In the morning, Jack knew, he'd have to check the Seattle Chinese directories.

For local traffic and news he powered on the television and caught an update on the Madrona Park shootings: three juvenile gangbangers had robbed and shot up an indoor hydroponic marijuana farm not far from the golf course.

Two dead. Two wounded, critically. And the report confirmed that one of the dead had indeed been the son of a city councilman.

The news program followed with a special presentation about new-age pot growers in the Emerald Triangle of the Northwest. He turned off the TV.

He took out the evidence from the 0-Five and spread the array of data along the edge of his bed. Eddie's juvenile poster and gang information. The little gray .22-caliber slug. There was a photo, and a note listing the serial numbers of the Rado and Movado wristwatches taken from the victims.

The story the Boston Chinese kid caught in the traffic stop had told him echoed in his ears. Was the Seattle connection just pure bullshit?

Jack considered visiting the local Chinese associations, but decided not to blow his cover yet. He didn't want to warn them off by broadcasting his investigation. Check the streets, Billy had advised; street guys always wind up back on the street.

He felt thirsty and drained one of the little bottles of vodka from the minibar. He opened the White Pages and spread the maps on the carpet. He resisted a second bottle as he drew a big circle around the International District and West Seattle. As he started plotting the businesses and addresses he wondered how much of a Chinaman's chance his investigation really had.

Hoping for a call from Seattle PD, he fell asleep thinking about red balls and yellow killers.

Cleansing

The Spa Garden, with its mix of fake and real greenery, its soft wood tones, and its cheery check-in counter, had seemed more like a yoga or fitness club than the glorified massage parlor that it was.

Mona had estimated that the spa was roughly a half-mile walk from her basement place on James Street, a trek that brought her to Union Place just under the freeway. She considered the walk as exercise, the air clean and revitalizing, a way to energize her legs and lungs. The walk would be followed by a two-hour session at the spa that consisted of thirty minutes reflexology, thirty minutes deep massage (neck and shoulders), ten minutes hot whirlpool, thirty minutes sauna/steamroom/shower, capped off with a healthy chirashi salad and Relaxation green tea from the on-site commissary.

The spa was the one indulgence she allowed herself, a ritual she brought from New York, the need to cleanse her body and also dissolve the toxins in her spiritual heart.

She kept a fresh change of clothes, and $666 in cash in her locker.

She'd jog the half mile back, then visit Chinatown to replenish her provisions.

The Spa Garden, as Mona quickly discovered, was Taiwanese-owned and operated. The facility provided a range of services, from facials to manicures and pedicures, from massage to waxing, and could readily manage eight clients during peak times. There were two large steam-room units and three hot tubs, and the manager, a fortyish Taiwanese woman, spoke enough Cantonese in response to Mona's clipped Mandarin that they'd been able to set up a membership plan.

Mona planned to dedicate two hours a week to the spa but was unsure about how many months she'd use the services. She signed up for a monthly membership instead of an annual plan. Cash, of course.

Many of the clients were Caucasian women, which conveniently allowed Mona to keep her distance, playing up her inability to speak English. "No speakee Englee," she'd learned to say.

The Garden also featured a backyard sundeck that opened onto a view of a waterfront park. The deck included three round tables under large red beach umbrellas, a vantage point that looked out over Elliott Bay.

Water Becomes Water

She caressed the charm even as the masseuse's strong fingers worked the soles of her feet, pressed into her neck and back, even as hot water and steam drew her blood to the skin's surface. The heated red jade bangle seemed to glow in the hot mist.

It was the deep massage that cleared the tension and the bad *chi* from her muscles, that broke up the knots across her shoulders, but it was the steam that drove the demons from her soul.

Water over water, whispered the charm. Have faith, journey forth through sacrifice.

As if the steam, the bubbling whirlpool, could purge the poisons inside her, poisons more spiritual than physical, as if heat could melt away her painful memories.

The spa was a form of exorcism and Buddhist salvation, the steamy rise of mercy and goodness from the depths inside her. *Forgiveness* releasing the anger, hate, bitterness. Like a devotee she rubbed steam off the hot charm of her mother's soul, dangling from her bracelet, dripping its secrets.

Water over Mountain. She took a shallow swallow of steam. *Beware troubles from the Northeast.*

It came as no surprise, but she hadn't expected the warning so soon.

Time, she believed, was still on her side.

Prayers

As Mona became more familiar with King Street, *Wong Daai gaai*, on her trips through Chinatown, she discovered a Buddhist temple, a humble storefront location that was unlike the grand temples and monasteries she'd visited in Hong Kong but which attracted a faithful following nonetheless.

The Lantern Festival, *Yuen Siu*, had already passed, but the temple had posted an announcement of ceremonies for the Spring Blessing Festival, and upcoming celebrations of Kwoon Yum's birthday, the coming of the Goddess of Mercy.

Inside, the monks and sisters wore burgundy-colored robes, led by a *sifu*, master, who wore a colorful dragon vest over the robe. The big room was hazy from the burning sticks of incense, and crowded, with a chanting drone that filled the air.

At the altar, Mona placed offerings of gladioli and fruits she'd bought in Chinatown, then touched fire to incense, which she stuck into an urn of packed ashes. She got on her knees before the large Buddha figurines and bowed her head into the cushions on the floor, picturing her deceased mother behind closed eyes. She mouthed a series of silent prayers in her mother's memory.

Afterward, as a further expression of love, she gave a generous donation to the monk sister, who appeared mildly surprised.

"Please remember my mother in your prayers," Mona requested.

"What is her name?" asked the sister. "We can post it at the altar."

"Please just pray for *all* mothers," Mona said, "during *ching ming*, memorial observances, and on Mother's Day."

The monk sister nodded acknowledgement, placed her hands together pointed toward Heaven, and bowed.

Mona returned the bow, then left the temple, with a heart less burdened by the weight of everlasting sorrow, with the droning *nom mor nom mor nom mor or may tor fut* trailing behind her.

Peace.

Siu Lam Sandal

Of average height and slight build, Tsai had been a student of *Shaolin Hung*-style boxing, and had honed his knife-combat skills. From his appearance, no one could suspect he was an experienced fighter, better at hand-to-hand than most of the number 49-rank thugs, but the martial arts above all had taught him the lesson of patience.

For three months now he had fielded reports from the ranks of fellow Grass Sandals in other American Chinatowns where the Red Circle had members or triad affiliates. Their leads had not panned out in Washington, Boston, Philadelphia, Miami, Chicago, Detroit, or Columbus. He hadn't expected much from those communities but had been hopeful that something would turn up in Houston, Dallas, Los Angeles, San Francisco, Seattle, Sacramento, Fremont, or Monterey Park. Even Anchorage, or Honolulu.

Tsai knew that Paper Fan would not be pleased, but the *bok ji sin* was a patient man as well, and had faith in his many subordinates. Time, the 415 leader knew, was a continuum that governed all things, and patience was part of that balance.

None of the discreet inquiries at Chinese jewelry stores had proven fruitful, yet he was sure the stolen items would turn up. No luck during the Lantern Festivals, either. Tsai knew that most of the Buddhist temples would have an established membership of true believers who worshipped regularly, but the monks would welcome visitors and new members, recording their donations in a sign-in log. Greeting visitors with shaved heads bowed, the monks would thank new worshippers for their offerings, and include them in their evening prayers. The monks also taught that patience was a virtue, and that justice, like vengeance, traveled in a circle. What goes around, mused Tsai, comes around.

He continued to advise vigilance, maintaining focus on the diamonds, or the gold, but not forgetting religion, or the myriad Chinatowns.

As per Paper Fan, of course.

Jack had left the motel early, taking a car service north to Pioneer Square. He'd planned to check out the pawnshops there first, before working his way back down to the locations he'd listed inside the big five-mile circle he'd drawn around the International District. Along the way he'd hoped to grab a *dim sum* snack in Chinatown while keeping a daylight eye out for *ma lo* Eddie.

Jack also thought he'd drop by the West Precinct again.

As the car cut through the brittle Seattle morning, Jack reflected. Pawnshops were businesses where desperate people, down on their luck, went to trade in valued pieces of their lives for lesser sums of money. These shops were also places where the thrifty-minded sought good bargains, and where thieves often went to fence their stolen goods.

The pawnshops on Jack's list went by different types of names, which were clues to the class of clientele they catered to. PIONEER GOLD EXCHANGE. CAPITOL CASH. USA PAWN. ELLIOTT BAY BROKERS. JOHNNY'S JEWELRY. BRIDGE BROTHER'S TRADING. FAMILY CAPITAL. SEATTLE GOLD AND SILVER. There were a dozen places where Jack hoped to pull a lucky hit on stolen Rado watches. What was Eddie going to do, eat them?

The first three places around Pioneer Square were clearly directed at the tourist trade, with big picture windows offering an array of glittering jewelry and fancy cameras. The watches were European style: Franck Mullers, Piagets, Breitlings and Tag Heuers. None of the store managers had done business with any Chinese lately, and they were always wary of Hong Kong knockoffs anyway. Jack canvassed those stores in less than an hour, and left the area just as the tourists started rolling in.

Two shops farther south in the I.D. carried plenty of gold jewelry and coins from Chinese customers, but no watches. Nearby, he came upon the Jade Pagoda café and the Golden Wok. He grabbed a quick cup of *nai cha* tea at the Pagoda, washing down two plates of *ha gow,* shrimp dumplings, and *lor bok go,* radish cakes, as he watched the main drag wake to the morning. Many Chinese people passed by, but none short enough to match Eddie's low profile.

Jack rode a bus south, past the Kingdome and toward the next cluster of pawnbrokers. When he passed a stretch of railroad yards his cell phone buzzed out a number he didn't recognize. The voice identified himself as Detective Nicoll of the Seattle Headquarters Squad.

"Thanks for calling—," Jack began.

"Well, I've been up for twenty-eight hours but let me understand this right," Nicoll said. "You're looking for a four and a half foot tall *Chinaman?* Not a *suspect?* Not a *fugitive?*"

Jack bit his tongue on *Chinaman* and answered, "He's a person of interest, actually."

"And your name?" Nicoll continued. "*Yoo,* was it? What's that, Korean?"

"Chinese," Jack answered sharply.

There was a pregnant pause.

"You realize we're on a red ball here?" asked Nicoll.

"Yeah," Jack replied. "It's all over the news."

"Yeah, so tell you what," Nicoll said with a sigh. "I'll notify Patrol again, see if they run across anything. He's a shorty, right?"

"Correct. And I appreciate the lookout," Jack added.

"Try me after the red ball," Nicoll said wearily before hanging up.

Chinaman still rang in Jack's brain. He could already imagine the jokes coming out of Patrol ranks: No shit. A short Chinaman? That's the entire male population of Chinatown! Or, Whaddya kidding me? Midget Chinaman? A dinky chinky? A short slant?

Jack didn't like getting the brush-off even though he understood SPD had their hands full with the double homicide, and were under political pressure as well. Cop-world was full of that setup.

At the end of the railroad yards, Jack found Johnny's Jewelry on a street of old storefronts beneath the highway. Johnny, a grizzled old man, looked at Eddie's juvie photo and said, "Nah. We get mostly Mexicans here. And a few of the *brothers,* occasionally. Besides, you guys all look alike anyways." He flashed a yellowed gap-toothed grin. "Know what I'm saying?"

Jack sighed as Johnny offered, "You try Chinatown?"

It started to rain again.

Three blocks away was Family Capital, where the proprietor was a cheerful middle-aged white woman who greeted Jack like he was the first customer of the day. Jack badged her and explained the scenario involving high-end watches. He didn't want to show Eddie's dated ten-year-old juvie poster because it had already confused people.

125

The shop had a glass display counter with shelves of watches, but no Rados.

"We got a ladies' black-face Movado recently," she offered.

Jack became alert. "From a Chinese?" he asked. "A short man?"

"No, from a Mexican," she said with a pause. "But there was a Chinese with him. Well, *Asian* anyway."

"Short?" Jack repeated.

"Oh yes," she recalled. "I thought he was a kid at first. Because of his height. But it was the Mexican, *Latino,* who offered the watch." She removed it from the counter.

It was a ladies' gold watch featuring a black dial with gold hands and the trademark concave dot. It came fixed onto a gold bangle bracelet that had a locking clasp. The styling was elegant, sophisticated. The back of the watchcase bore the Movado logo SINCE 1881 laser-printed across the top. In the center was a line of eight numbers and letters, indicating the style; beneath which ran the serial number, consisting of seven digits. Across the bottom were the words SAPPHIRE CRYSTAL.

Jack jotted down the numbers. "What did he look like?" he asked.

"The Mexican?"

"No, the Chinese, *Asian*, first."

"Well, he wore glasses. Like a student, that's what I thought. He looked around at the camera counter. Never said a word."

Eyeglasses, noted Jack suspiciously, realizing the ruse. White people didn't focus much attention on Chinese anyway, other than, "They all look alike, know what I'm saying?"

If Eddie donned a pair of nerdy drugstore eyeglasses, he'd really be invisible. Except for his height. Eddie couldn't disguise *that*.

"The Mexican man, he was a little older, in his thirties, I guess," the woman continued. "He had a thin mustache, I think. He said he bought the watch down in L.A. for his girlfriend. But then they broke up. He said he needed the money for rent, so he was pawning it." She wiped the watch with a soft cloth, admiring it. "Amorosa," she said, referring to the watch series. "He said that his girlfriend was named Rosa. And he had picked this one because it meant 'love Rosa.' I felt bad for him. I gave him my top offer."

"How much did he get?" Jack asked.

"About a hundred fifty," she said. "That model retails for about six hundred. We'll resell for three hundred, thereabouts."

"A hundred fifty, that's all he got?" Jack asked skeptically.

"That's it. We *do* have a mark-up policy."

Jack took a photo of the Movado, using his plastic disposable camera, and recopied the serial numbers. "Can I see the transaction information?" Jack asked.

"Will I take a loss?" she asked warily. "If the watch turns out to be stolen?"

"I'm not after the watches," Jack assured her. "I promise, no loss."

She produced a ledger, from which he copied the name "Carlos Lima," and the address "44 South Andover." There was no telephone number.

"Thanks," Jack smiled. "I'll be in touch if anything turns up."

"And *you* have a nice day," she replied, as he went back out into the rain.

There were more pawnshops on the list, and he felt the chess game was just beginning.

The first pawnshop on South Spokane was another small storefront with racks of rings and necklaces in the front window. Jack could see that the young white man inside was on the phone, occasionally glancing out at the street. There was a counter of assorted folding knives.

Jack noticed a wall display of watches as the man buzzed him in. "Look around," the man said. "Let me know if you need help."

Jack smiled and said okay as the man ended his phone conversation in a language Jack didn't recognize. Slavic. Polish, Eastern European. He scanned over the array of watches, and saw it right away. On the middle shelf, the ladies' Movado with the black-face dial.

"That one," said Jack. "Can I see it?"

"Certainly," the man said, placing the tray on the counter between them. Jack turned the watch over and checked the serial number. It was eight digits off from the Movado previously pawned at Family Capital. Two identical watches eight numbers apart? At the end of a series of seven numbers? Same batch, he figured.

The watch had a $400 tag on it.

Jack decided to badge the man, assuring him he wasn't after the watch.

"When did you acquire this?" Jack asked. "And from whom?"

"It was one of the Chicanos," he said. "Three or four weeks ago."

"He was alone?"

"Yes, he sold the watch."

Jack gave him a puzzled look.

"There was a *Japanese* man, *Chinese* man, whatever, with him," the man said. "But he waited outside."

"Outside the door?" Jack asked. "Was it raining then?"

"It rains all the time here." The man smirked. "I don't remember about then. He walked up and down the street. I only glimpsed him for a few moments."

"What makes you think they were together?" Jack asked.

"Not me. My nephew, Vlady, returning from his lunch break. He saw them way down the street. The Chicano man was giving the cash to the short Chinese man, he said."

Short, Jack noted. "I need the name."

The man produced a notebook, thumbed it until he got to the entry: MOVADO, LADY, WATCH. $125 JORGE VILLA. The next entry: 44 S. ANDOVER. The same crib as Carlos Lima.

"This Chicano," Jack asked, "did he say where he's from?"

"Los Angeles. He bought the watch for his girlfriend. But they broke up." He shrugged like it was an old story. "He needed the money for rent."

"Did he say what the girlfriend's name was?" asked Jack.

The man paused, his eyes narrowing. "Rosita. Rosa something. It was the Amorosa series; he said it sounded like her name."

"Thanks," Jack said, knowing he needed to check one more shop on Spokane before heading toward South

Andover. At the very least, he thought, it was a good lead to pass on to Seattle PD.

Closer to Highway 99, he came upon an old warehouse building that had a run-down storefront on the street. Above its dingy picture window was an American flag and a red, white, and blue sign that announced USA TRADERS GOLD, GUNS, GUITARS.

A small surveillance camera was perched above the doorway.

Looking beyond the trays of jewelry and the pair of lacquered Stratocasters featured in the window, Jack could see a display of weapons and more guitars in the background.

He pressed the button on the door, heard laughter from inside, and waited a long time before he was buzzed in. The man nearest the door had a high-and-tight military haircut; he watched Jack with narrow blue eyes, displaying a crooked smile. He wore a Guns N' Roses wifebeater shirt and a black leather wristband. Farther in, another man stood behind a long counter perusing a *Motorcycle* magazine. He wore his dark grungy hair long, folded his hairy arms across his Harley-Davidson T-shirt. There was a gun in the holster on his hip.

"You have watches?" Jack asked.

The man nodded toward the far corner, and Jack passed a display counter of Magnum revolvers but there were no small-caliber pieces. A selection of semiautomatic pistols reminded Jack of the guns used at Lucky's OTB shoot-out. On the wall was a shelf of assault rifles, and a display of swords and knives. The far wall featured a half dozen electric guitars, an *Easy Rider* movie poster, and a blow-up concert picture of Kurt Cobain. There was another counter of

Las Vegas–type jewelry: gaudy gold-and-diamond-encrusted rings and bracelets, platinum medallions in the shape of dollar signs, lucky horseshoes, and dice.

Then he saw the display case of wristwatches.

"Can I see this one?" Jack asked.

The biker man took his time coming over, lazily sliding the watch tray onto the glass countertop. Jack saw the same Movado Amorosa model with a $375 tag on it. Checking the back of the watch, Jack saw that the serial number followed the one supplied by "Carlos Lima" exactly. Beyond coincidence, Jack knew.

"It's real all right," the man said. "No need to check."

"Did you get this from an Asian person?" Jack asked.

"Say what?" the man responded through a frown. Jack badged him, and explained that he wasn't after the watch, but the person who sold it.

"Why didn't you identify yourself sooner?" the man complained.

"Wouldn't have been necessary," Jack said bluntly, "if you didn't have this watch."

The man shook his head disdainfully and said, "It wasn't no Asian. It was a *beaner*. A Mexicano."

"There was a little Jap with him," the other man interjected. Jack glanced at him, saw the grin on his face. "Yeah," the man continued, "they came in together. The little Jap, or Chink, whatever." He was trying to get a rise out of Jack. "He went looking at the gun wall. I told him, 'Don't bother, you need to be eighteen for guns.'"

Jack played it cool. "He was short, so you thought he was a kid?"

"A Mongolian runt, right." He grinned.

"What did he look like?" Jack grinned back.

"Who knows? They all look alike to me." A sneer marred his face.

"He didn't say anything?"

"Probably couldn't speak English. He just walked away, waited outside."

"But it was the *wetback* who sold it," the counterman joined in.

Jack took a step back and said, "I need to see the documents."

The men straightened up, indignant. "What documents?"

"The paperwork," Jack said evenly. "The *pawnee* information."

No one was grinning anymore.

"Wait a minute, man," the biker said defiantly. "You ain't even Seattle PD. I don't have to show you nothing."

He might know someone on the force, guessed Jack.

"Go ahead, call SPD," he continued. "See if I care. I got rights. And shit, I got a business to run here. Go ahead, call 'em."

"Sure, I could do that," Jack said sharply. "It'd only take a few seconds." He placed the watch back on the tray. "But after they show up as a courtesy to a cop, I'm going to spend the day going over your inventory. I'm going to tie up your books, interrupt your business, your lunch, your dinner, everything. And keep you open late, so I hope you haven't made plans for the evening."

The man's face clenched into a look of hate. He took a

deep breath through his nose, spread his feet like he was getting ready to fight.

"Or," Jack offered, "you could just show me the name, the address, phone number, whatever. And my Asian ass will be out of here in two minutes."

The smart-ass rock star wannabe went over to the gun displays and kept quiet.

After a long moment, the biker glared at the watch, mouthing the word *fuck!* before replacing it into the display counter. "Why can't you people clean up your own shit," he bitched, "instead of harassing us *true* Americans?" He was still spewing hate as he stepped away into a tiny office.

Jack stood in a neutral spot and waited until the biker reappeared with a sheet of entries, information from a Seattle non-driver ID, a copy of a green card. Jack jotted down the information, memorized the likeness of the Mexican seller. He imagined the shadow of short Eddie in the background.

Jack could feel the men staring daggers into his back as he left the USA shop. He remembered Alex and knew he should leave her a message. *Sorry, lady. Let's try for later tonight.* Turning up his collar, he headed for 44 South Andover.

Mona had gone daily to the Chinese employment agency, a little cutout storefront near King Street that featured a wall of paper tickets on which various types of jobs were offered. She pretended to be a job seeker, and discovered most of the ads were for busboys, dishwashers, kitchen help. A few for laborers, grist for the construction trades. Some tickets for sweatshops.

Many of the seekers were Fukienese by dialect, but she'd understood a little of whatever Mandarin she overheard. Most of the seekers were in transit to other places, *Say nga touh*, Seattle, being only their first destination.

She'd have a cup of *nai cha* tea after each visit, at the Fuzhou Garden bakery across the street, still watching the little employment agency storefront.

The third week, Mona noticed her, a Chinese woman about the same height and weight as herself. Mona knew the woman's eyes would be brown, and the hair color didn't really matter. Age could be altered by a mask of calculated makeup, and besides, it was often difficult to guess the age of Chinese people.

Mona struck up a conversation with the woman, and over *yum cha* tea at the Fuzhou Garden, discovered that she had emigrated under a guest worker program visa, and had worked as a nanny for a Chinese couple in the Queen Anne neighborhood, who had a two-year-old child and also required housekeeping duties.

After almost six months, the husband had come on to her, pressing her for sex, and the wife had wound up firing her. She had considered working for Caucasians, the *gwailo*, but her English wasn't any good.

Jing Su Tong was five foot two, 118 pounds. *Yat yat bot. Yat bok yat sup bot.* Sure to prosper, sure to grow. Twenty-eight years old. Perfect. She had straight shoulder-length black hair, with some partial bangs across her forehead.

Mona knew she could copy the look, could forge a realistic resemblance. The height and weight, approximately. Most customs workers appeared to feel that Asians all resembled each other anyway.

Jing Su had been hoping for work as a home-care attendant in Chinatown but hadn't seen any such jobs posted. Her savings were being depleted and she was becoming desperate; her family in China needed her monthly contributions. She was considering going to San Francisco where she had relatives.

Appearing sympathic, Mona explained that her own tourist visa had expired, and wondered if they couldn't help each other. She offered Jing Su five thousand dollars in cash in exchange for her Social Security card, non-driver's identification card, and employment documents. Offering her too much would arouse Jing Su's suspicions, thought Mona, but if she offered too little, the woman would ask for more anyway. Being firm was best. Five thousand dollars would cover the woman's efforts to find work, enable her to send some money back home, and tide her over for at least three months. After that, she could report her cards lost or stolen, and some *Wah chok wui*, some Chinese service center, would help her get them reissued.

By then, Mona had planned to be long gone.

Jing Su accepted Mona's offer, of course. To her, renting her papers for three months was a godsend. Buy time, find work, family in China. "*Mo mon tay*," she declared. "No problem."

No problem, thought Mona. If only it were true.

But the new identity was a ticket out.

The *way* of freedom.

Back in her James Street sanctuary Mona blew the steam off the Iron Goddess tea, caressed the jade charm in her palm, ran her fingernails over the *bot gwa* Taoist trigrams. *Bok* she'd touched. *North*. Mountains. *Mountain over Water*. The Chinese word for blindness came to mind—*Beware the woman who sees the gold and not the man. Nothing good will come of it.*

Blindness.

Childlike *naïveté*.

Yet *all goes well?*

She paused, unsure how to interpret this. *Naïveté* could lead to danger, but *all goes well?* She took a deep sip of the Iron Goddess.

Move forward, she resolved.

The way of freedom.

She looked at the large sack of jasmine rice propped up in the corner near the rice cooker. Plenty, she'd told the old couple, don't stand on ceremony. Just ask if you need some.

She remembered the folktale about villagers hiding a fortune inside the rice barrels. What thief would suspect a fortune hidden in plain sight? But she knew that inside the rice sack, buried near the bottom, was a mahjong case full of gold Panda coins, diamonds, and jewelry. More than a quarter million dollars' worth.

Soon she'd have a safe deposit box and wouldn't have to take such risks.

She knew she had to be careful selling the coins and diamonds. Dumping the whole lot at once would draw the wrong type of attention, and lessen the value as well. There was enough cash to tide her over until she could set up the bank accounts. Gradually, she'd sell some of her cache, and offer a pair of diamonds, a few coins, to test the waters. An American gold firm that employed American-born Chinese, *jook sings*, could be useful. Less chance of a connection to the triads.

Perhaps it would lead to more opportunities; the American-born cared more about the markup than where the gold and jewels came from. Besides, she believed her new identity would shield her. After all, Chinese families sold off jewelry and gold all the time.

Or may tor fut. She whispered the Buddhist chant, rubbing the jade between her palms. Her fingers crossed the hexagrams as she read *Heaven Over Lake*. An escape route opens. Be mindful of small steps, and there can be safety even on dangerous ground. Tread *around* the tiger's tail.

Savoring the Cherry

Gee Sin powered off the bionic hand, lest its electric murmur intrude, spoiling the mood of the expected debauchery.

A female *cho hai*, a new Grass Sandal, 432 rank, had selected them from an aspiring pimp, Kowloon Charlie, who'd guaranteed the girls were at least seventeen years old, even if they could easily pass for fourteen. Two *siu jeer*, "young ladies," recruited from the impoverished zones and orphanages: the poor, the desperate, forsaken children. Gee Sin knew Grass Sandal would never place Paper Fan in jeopardy, given Hong Kong's rigid underage prostitution–human trafficking laws. And the continuing police efforts targeting him. It was difficult to guess a young whore's age anyway, he thought, even if you were Chinese and knew the clues.

Gee Sin also knew Kowloon Charlie had a growing interest in the triad's prostitution rackets; he was an up-and-coming *gai wong,* pimp player, whom competing triads wanted to lure away. Or kill outright. Kowloon Charlie had been eager to please, to fulfill Paper Fan's requests. Charlie had the best whores, and for the time being, nobody had wanted to bring the vice dogs from the Royal Hong Kong Police down into the lucrative operations, especially in *Tshim Sha Tsui.*

Sin motioned with his quiet arm, directing both girls into his bedroom. "*Chue som,*" he said in a low voice. Get undressed.

The first one would have been the age of a grand-daughter if he'd had one: short, but *Bok bok jeng jeng*, with light skin and pretty, sweet with long black hair. She offered a crooked half-smile and a look of resignation as she stripped. She had small breasts with thick nubby nipples, but they were nicely shaped, he thought, and made her appear more juvenile. A waifish body, hardly any hips, but her backside was rounded and plump. *Gow leng*, cute enough.

Naked, she lay down on the bed, placed a thick pillow under her rear. She put one hand into her hair and fanned it across the comforter, extending her pink high heels toward the bed corners. She spread her knees open with her free hand.

The other girl was darker, ethnic Chinese from Southeast Asia, he'd guessed. Malaysia, Indonesia—he couldn't tell which. Dark, silver-dollar nipples. Also short, barely five foot two, but with curves everywhere on her: a firm, virginal, country-girl body.

She'd been wearing a schoolgirl's uniform, with a white see-through bra and a split-thong underneath.

He unbuckled his belt. Unzipped his fly.

Naked, she sat on the rear edge of his bed, with the other *siu jeer* behind her, and raised one leg, leaning back on her hands. Gee Sin stepped up to the bed, took a breath, sucking in the *hom sup* salty scent of the sex flesh splayed before him.

"*Gway day,*" he said softly to the dark-skinned one, *kneel,* just before he let his trousers drop.

She knelt down on the beige carpeting, slowly reaching for

him as he leaned over the bed. He was bracing himself on his spread fingers, his attention turning to the one on his bed.

He was mesmerized by the hairless vulva, *yum bo*, fleshy labia, *yum soon*, cutaneous folds spreading toward *soon hut*, the hooded little pearl. Devouring the glistening pudendum with his lustful eyes.

He lowered his head, close enough that he could smell the sweet muskiness emanating from her.

She kept her eyes on him and slowly arched her back.

The one on her knees had tugged down his shorts and taken hold of him in her hands, caressing the swelling *look go,* tube of flesh. He noticed the faint mound of downy hair just above the hooded lips, the mons, below *nymphae* nestled there.

He dry-swallowed, marveling at the *bo*, orifice, beckoning to him, an old man in his twilight, drinking at the fountain of youth. It made him feel like a young man again, when he had *two* good hands, and touching a woman brought a lusty tingle to his fingertips.

The *siu jeer* on the carpet cradled his swollen *gwun* against her cheek, strummed her fingers across the taut balls beneath it.

He'd lost his bearings.

His legs began to tremble as he bent close enough to blow gently on the *bo* pearl, to gasp a hot breath onto it. He was caught in its spell. The tip of his tongue would make it hard, bring it to attention. Precious, *bo*. Worshipping at the orifice of precious pudendum. Labia. *Yum soon.*

Licking his lips in anticipation.

South Andover ran between two sets of railroad tracks, trapped inside the industrial spread and the freeway beyond, a beat-down neighborhood.

Number 44 was one of a forsaken inner-city string of row houses that'd fallen into disrepair. Now it was a rooming house for migrant workers, makeshift quarters, beds for rent in squalid conditions. It reminded Jack of the Fukienese crash pads along East Broadway where modern-day worker-coolies were stacked on top of one another in basements and tenement apartments.

Jack knocked on the door until someone answered, opening up cautiously to a shadowy interior of whispers and furtive faces.

"Si, que quiere?" asked a young face creased with wrinkles.

Jack showed his badge, said *"Policia de Nueva York. No inmigracion."* Jack assured him, *"No problema.* I only have some questions for Carlos Lima. And Jorge Villa."

There was a silence as the door opened wider and another Mexican man stepped forward. "Si," he said. *"Soy Jorge."*

"Jorge," Jack began, "you sold two watches that were stolen—"

"No, no, *senor,*" interrupted Jorge. "I no stealin nossing, please."

"I don't care about the watches," Jack insisted.

"No me. *Fue el chino bajo*," Jorge said. "*Chino malo, el chaparrito.*"

Bajo, remembered Jack. *Short*, short Chinese. Eddie was fronting the watches? "Where?" Jack asked. "*Donde?*"

"No say. He calling, *telefono*, only."

"Where did you meet him?" Jack scanned the dim hushed room. "And where is Carlos Lima?"

Comida Mexicana

Jack brought Jorge along and they followed the freeway back north to Holgate until they came to a fast-food restaurant next to a Metro bus stop. El Amigo offered a counter with stools and four small tables inside an old-time diner. There was an oven and grill setup with a microwave on one side, then a big steam table with pots of beans, sides, and assorted ingredients.

El Amigo served *pozole, lengua*, and tacos ten ways, with a full menu of burritos, tortillas, enchiladas, fajitas. Flan and sopaipillas for dessert. TAKEOUT ORDERS, DELIVERY FREE.

The place was empty this mid-afternoon, except for the grill cook. The savory aromas that wafted into the cold air pulled them inside.

"Carlos," Jorge said to the cook. "*Policia*."

A look of fear crossed Carlos's face before Jack assured him, "*No problema*, bro."

Jack showed him Eddie's juvenile offender photograph.

Carlos paused, taking a good look at Jack before he spoke. "*Chaparrito*," he said, referring to the photo. "He say hees work for hees oncle, *jewree*." Carlos pointed to the Mexican ring on his finger, to the matching chain and medallion around his neck.

Jewelry store. Jack listened, knew it was Eddie running a story.

"He say beesnees *no esta bueno, esta cerrado*," Carlos continued. "Hees oncle pays him *con los relojes. Entiende?*" He tapped his finger on the knockoff Cartier tank on his wrist. "*El chino bajo,* he say we help him selling dem, then he geev us twenny dollar for one."

"You get a twenty-dollar commission?" asked Jack.

"*Si.* He make up story for *los gringos.* Me and Jorge, we no stealing nossing."

Jack took a moment to piece it together in his mind. They had sold the Movados to the pawnshops near the railroad yards and on Spokane because those places were closest to their immigrant rooming house on South Andover. Or had *bajo chaparrito*—Eddie—planned to steer clear of the upscale tourist destinations? Instead keeping to the low-rent areas, and drawing less attention? A heavyset man wearing a polo shirt came out of a back room, saw Jack, and asked, "*Si? Hay un problema?*"

"*No problema,*" Jack answered. "You're the owner?"

"*Si,* and these are my best workers. And I know they never steal anything."

"I'm not after them," Jack insisted. "I'm only asking them about their Chinese *amigo,* who they said they met here."

"Chinese?" he paused, puzzled, glancing from Jorge to Carlos. "You mean Koo Lung?"

Koo? thought Jack, recalling Koo Jai, Eddie's victim in New York. "Who's Koo Lung?" He showed the juvie photo, and asked, "He look something like this? Very short?"

"*Chino chaparrito,*" the man said, nodding. "He worked here for one week."

"Why? What happened?" quizzed Jack.

"He saw the sign for dishwasher job in the window. But I also made him clean out the basement and paint the back room. And he didn't like to make deliveries."

Working him like a coolie, thought Jack.

"Too much work, he said. He wanted to be dishwasher only, so he quit."

"Dishwasher *only?*"

"We *say* dishwasher," the man said with a chuckle, "but really it's *garbage worker*. And includes fix-up work, dirty work. Carlos and Jorge are good cooks, best in Puebla. Six days on, one day off. They don't have time for the dirty work. Or deliveries."

"This Koo Lung," Jack asked. "You have any paperwork on him?"

"Only the job application. It's just a formality."

"*Por favor,*" Jack said. "I need to see it."

The job application form listed the applicant as KOO K. LEUNG. There was an address in Central Seattle with a telephone number. Attached was a copy of a membership card from ASIAN VIPs NYC; Jack guessed it was a hostess club. Eddie had ripped off his victim Koo Jai's card and used it as ID.

"This the only identification you got?" asked Jack.

"*El chinito* said he got robbed. Lost everything, except *that.*"

Jack flashed him a look of disbelief.

"It was only a formality anyway." The man shrugged. "Something for the labor inspectors."

Jack called the telephone number and got a recording announcing service had been canceled. He copied the address off the application and called a car service to Central Seattle.

Carlos said, "*El chaparrito no esta bueno,* no good. He shoot me pool, *billar.* He win me *engañando.*"

"Billiards?" Jack asked. "He hustled you? Where?"

"Donde viven los filipinos." He gave Jack a crumpled newsletter from his pocket. A community center in Filipinotown.

"Gracias," Jack said, giving Carlos his NYPD PBA card. "Call me if he comes here looking for you."

Carlos and Jorge nodded as Jack went to the cab that had pulled up outside.

The address that Eddie had submitted turned out to be an administrative office building not far from the University District, on Summit near East Madison, closer to the market. Give a university location, figured Jack, and people took you for a student, especially if you were Asian. Part of the disguise.

A bogus address, a dead end.

Jack caught another cab to Filipinotown.

The Villamor Community Center was closed by the time Jack arrived. A schedule posted on the main door noted that the center was closed on Sundays as well. Another dead end.

Jack wasn't far from Chinatown and decided to calm the gnawing hunger in his gut.

Jade Garden was one of the restaurants he hadn't visited, so he stopped in for a plate of beef and tomatoes over noodles. He peeped the kitchen, hoping to see someone very short. Again, no luck. While he waited, a news bulletin about the red ball homicides was broadcast from a television set above the cashier's counter. They'd arrested two suspects. Teenagers. He called the West Precinct. Detective Nicoll was still out, and Jack wondered whether he was finally getting some sleep.

Devouring the dish of noodles, he recalled the details of his investigation into Nicoll's voice mail: the watches and pawnshops, the Mexicans, the bogus information, and, adding to the end of the list, he likes to shoot pool.

Jack knew he had only one more day in Seattle, and wondered how much more ground he could cover.

Overthrow the Ching

Alex nursed a martini as the master of ceremonies took the stage and quieted the audience for the ORCA Silent Auction. The CADS were among the hundreds of people in attendance, ready to bid on items for charitable Asian causes.

The first item up for bidding was an antique Chinese fan, reminiscent of the Ming Dynasty era. The white paper fan was made of bamboo and parchment, and had two thick outer ribs, bracing the thirteen accordion paper folds inside.

Alex took a sip of her cocktail and checked her watch.

"The fat ribs of the fan once represented the capitals of Peking and Nanking under the first Ming emperor. There are poems on both sides of the fan, believed to have been written by Dr. Sun Yat-sen himself. A white peony appears on the front of the fan, a red peony on the back. Turning the fan meant overthrowing the Ching Dynasty, and was a gesture of many secret societies." The master of ceremony paused to catch his breath.

Alex was curious about where Jack was, and wondered if he'd call after the auction. She knew that cop stuff ruled his world, and figured he'd gotten himself involved in more police trauma. She drained her drink as bidding for the fan commenced.

Cop Stuff

Back at the Sea-Tac Courtyard, Jack took a hot shower that steamed up the little room. It was almost 8 PM and he considered calling Alex. She'd said she'd be free after nine.

He changed into the fresh suit from the backpack, thinking he'd meet Alex at the Westin bar lounge after her Service Recognition Award Dinner ended. They could start with a couple of drinks while he tried to reel his mind away from the Eddie *monkey* chase.

His cell phone buzzed. Alex hooking up, he thought.

But the voice was pale male, law enforcement. "Detective Yu?"

"Yeah," Jack answered. "Who's this?"

"SPD Patrol, sir." Professional.

"What have you got?" asked Jack, swallowing.

"We have in custody a person of interest to you," the cop said. "Come to Manila Street and Walker. Just off the freeway."

The cab service dropped Jack off a block away from where the SPD cruiser sat, its lights out on the desolate street. The area was north of the motel, with highway noise humming in the distance. Jack approached and badged the driver, noticing that someone was in the backseat. One of the uniformed officers got out of the squad car and walked Jack a short distance away before he said, confidentially, "He said his name was Carl Lim, but he didn't have any ID. We saw him playing solo nine-ball when we rolled into Julio's Place on Manila Street. The patrol update was for a very short male, may shoot pool."

"Yeah, go on," said Jack, figuring the update was from Detective Nicoll.

"So we figured we'd bring him to the car, check him out. Okay. Once we leave Julio's and hit the street, he gets free and we gotta chase him, like six fuckin' blocks. Jimmy caught him first, took him down hard."

Jack nodded, an offer of respect and appreciation.

"He was uncooperative after that," the cop continued. "Started bitching police brutality." He gave Jack a business card that read JOON KOREAN GINSENG DISTRIBUTOR, with a Jackson Street address. "We found that on him. Nothing much else. Anyway, we can hold him for disorderly, resisting, or assault on a police officer. Anything like that, he's got at least a few days chillin' with the bad boys."

Jack understood that meant Eddie would be in custody a while, and since it was a weekend, it'd be harder to find a public defender even if he demanded one.

They turned back toward the cruiser.

"Bring him out," Jack said.

The man could have passed for a kid, short enough, his head well beneath Jack's chin.

"I was just shooting pool," the Chinese man protested, "I didn't do *anything*."

"Heard you did the marathon, trying to cut out." Jack

yanked down the shoulder of the man's jacket. Even in the dim street light, the Red Star tattoo was clearly visible.

"What the fuck," the man complained. "Yeah, I ran. Those *gwailo* cops were looking to fuck me over!"

"Okay, cut the bullshit," Jack said, pulling back the handcuffs to reveal a monkey tattoo on the man's wrist. Curious George. "This is *jing deng*," marveled Jack. Destiny.

"What's that?" puzzled Eddie.

Ngai jai dor gai, remembered Jack. Short people are shrewd.

"So what's your name again?" Jack pressed.

"Carl Lim."

Jack chuckled "You mean like in 'Carlos Lima'?"

The man's face froze.

"How about 'Jorge Villa'?" Jack challenged. "Who would you be then, George Hui? Curious George, huh?" Jack could see the man's resemblance to the face in the juvenile offender photo, and decided to bluff. "Guess what, Eddie?" Jack deadpanned. "Your own *dailo* placed you at OTB."

"Dailo?" sneered Eddie. "Bullshit."

"He said you guys had a beef over watches, and money," Jack prodded.

"Right. Last I heard," Eddie said defiantly, "he was brain dead in Emergency."

"Yeah, you keep believing that," Jack snapped. "He put your shorty ass at the scene. In the alley." Jack noticed Eddie flinch at being called "shorty." "That's right, you're *bad*," Jack added sarcastically, "so bad you're good for Murder One, monkey boy."

He pushed Eddie back into the cruiser, and took a better look at the Korean ginseng business card. The address was just off the fringe of Chinatown.

"Let's roll," Jack said as he slipped in beside Eddie.

Number 818 Jackson was on a street that slanted off the intersection of Jackson and Rainier, a quiet street this time of day. It was an old-style house with an addition built onto the back of it. There was a street-level back door that led inside.

An old Asian couple came out as the patrol car killed its flashing strobes.

Eddie stared at them from the backseat, his mouth quiet but his eyes scheming.

Jack came out of the cruiser and walked toward them. Korean, he guessed. The cops kept the cruiser's interior lights on so the old couple could see Eddie behind the back cage partition.

Eddie finally bowed and twisted his face away.

Jack showed the man the business card.

"*Ai goo,*" the old man said. "He rent room from us."

"Can I see the room?" Jack asked respectfully, offering a slight bow.

"*Ari seyo,*" the man agreed.

The inside hallway smelled like *bulgogi* and *kimchi,* with the menthol hint of *salon pas* drifting off the old couple. They led Jack to a side room. The small room had only enough space for a single bed with an all-purpose night table and a freestanding metal cabinet that doubled as a closet and a dresser. Some clothes were draped around a chair. No windows. No bathroom. Not many places to hide anything.

Jack considered the obvious: toss the bed, the cabinet, check the knapsack, and under the chair and night table. He gauged the concern on the faces of the Korean couple. Remembering the East Broadway railroad flat that Eddie and his victim Koo Jai had shared in New York's Chinatown, he pictured the loose floorboards covering their stash spots.

The floor here was covered with old linoleum, and Jack didn't see any loose edges or pried-up corners. He guessed Eddie was smarter than that. He heard a click, like a timer, then the hum of a fan unit nearby. Air. Since there were no windows, he looked for the vent, and saw the aluminum grate high on the wall, covering the extension of the ductwork into the room addition.

Too high up for Eddie to reach. Unless he stood on a chair.

Jack pulled the chair over, flashed his Mini Maglite into the grate. A shallow recess, empty. But there was a bend in the air duct. Although barely visible, he noticed a tiny plastic loop wrapped around the bottom slat of the vent grate. It looked like fishing line.

Jack opened his army penknife to the Phillips screwdriver and unscrewed the grate. It came free after a slight pry, but was caught on the nylon line. Jack tugged gently and saw a dirty plastic bundle emerge from the bend in the duct. He dragged it out and saw metallic watchbands inside. In one corner of the clear plastic bundle he could make out the denomination on a wad of fifty-dollar bills.

He unwrapped the plastic, then admired the expensive watches within: three Rolex Oysters, four Cartier Tanks, six

Rados. And five black-dial Movado Amorosas. Probably fifty grand's worth of deluxe timepieces, guessed Jack. He thumbed through the wad of cash, maybe five thousand, that had probably been ripped out of the victim's pants pocket as he lay dying in the snow of the Doyers Street alley.

Damn clever, thought Jack, turning to the old couple as he scanned the room again. "Where's the bathroom?"

Going back through the hallway, they came to a closet-size bathroom that consisted of a sink, a toilet, and a narrow shower stall with a sliding door and a vent fan in the ceiling.

Eddie was clever, Jack concluded, but in a predictable way.

Removing a roll of toilet tissue and a can of air freshener, Jack lifted the cover off the toilet's water tank. The water was murky and he shined the flashlight into it. At the bottom of the tank there was a roll of black plastic. The cold tank water had pressed the plastic into the contours of a gun.

Jack felt the chill of the water as he pulled it out.

Inside the black plastic was a revolver, a .22-caliber Taurus with a nine-shot cylinder. The murder weapon from the OTB shooting. Jack took a breath. It had barely taken him a half hour inside the Korean house. He knew some of his effort here bordered on illegal search and seizure but he didn't care. He had the killer, the murder weapon, and the swag all bundled up, just in need of a lab match for ballistics and forensics. What mattered was that the perpetrator was in custody, he thought. A lawyer, like Alex, might disagree, but Jack wasn't feeling the need to be legally correct at this exhilarating moment.

Eddie was somber as Jack leaned into the back window of the cruiser and said, "We've got the gun, kid. You're good, though, shooting .22s. A hitman's caliber. You're good for two kill-shots, and one critical hit."

"Don't know nothing about no gun," Eddie insisted.

"How long do you think before we match up the ballistics? Before your prints come back off the watches? And off the vic's VIP card from the titty bar, that you used for ID?" Jack shook his head dismissively.

Eddie grunted, smirked.

"What happened?" Jack needled. "You had a beef? Something over stolen watches? Come on, stop gassing me. It's not like you're going anywhere except to lockup. Right now, you're good for the possession of the firearm, for the possession of stolen goods. Probably good for Murder One as well."

"What the fuck is it to you anyway?" Eddie snapped. "The jerk-off scumbag had it coming."

"Oh yeah, I'm sure," agreed Jack. "But it's not *only* that you shot this Koo guy in the back. *And* robbed him. Or even the big Ghost gorilla you took out."

"What then?" was Eddie's pained question.

"You also put two .22s into the head of a guy I used to know," Jack said coldly. "It's *Yin-Yang*, punk, and yours has come full circle."

Jack turned to the patrol cop, asking, "How'd you make him?"

"We got the heads-up at roll call, for a Chinese," the cop smiled sheepishly. "*Exceptionally short*, right? The update said he liked to shoot pool."

"Good work," Jack commended him, privately noting Detective Nicoll's assistance.

"But if he hadn't run," the cop added, "we probably wouldn't have had reason to hold him."

"Thanks," Jack offered. "I owe you guys big time. Pick the bar, the tab's on me." He clutched the two bags of evidence he knew he'd have to voucher with SPD, and realized he'd also have to advise his New York precincts of his actions.

By the time Jack was done at Seattle Police Headquarters, it was eleven thirty, with much of the International District already shut down. His adrenaline carried him until he remembered Alex and her events at the Westin. He felt like celebrating, wanting to tell her about the day's investigations, the strenuous, dogged police work, then the collar. But he was too professional for that.

However, hooking up with her for drinks would be a treat, capping off a "mission accomplished" with a twist of *jing deng*, destiny.

He called Alex's room at the hotel, and was surprised to hear a man's voice. One of the CADS? Strangely, ADA Sing came to his mind. Music in the background. Caught off-guard, he quickly hung up, going back into his jacket to confirm her room number.

When he called again, the phone rang until he got the hotel voice-mail message. Hadn't Alex been rooming with Joann somebody? He decided not to leave a message, feeling conflicted, wanting to consider it just an innocent miscommunication.

After all, it wasn't like they'd agreed to meet. He tried to downplay it. She was probably out with the ladies, the staffers. The uncertainty irked him and he didn't know why, but he felt the fatigue of the long day setting in, and decided to return to the motel. He knew Alex still had one more day of the convention, and he hoped to see her at the gala finale.

Back at the motel room he sucked down four of the little bottles of vodka from the minibar, sitting at the window watching the night rain splatter against the glass. He thought about the fancy watches and the nine-shot revolver and the cold-blooded little man who'd shown no signs of remorse.

He thought about Alex, and all the rain checks, until the alcohol reached his brain and closed his mind.

Change

The Phoenix Garden Beauty Salon occupied the second floor of an office building on a Chinatown side street. The local spa spot offered the usual haircuts and facials, manicures and pedicures. Three massage tables were neatly hidden in the rear rooms.

The big front room was all chrome and mirrors, filled by the roar of blow-dryers and buzzing clippers, and a chemical smell of baking electrifying the air. Hong Kong pop music played in the background intermittently, a jittery cacophony. Six hair stations lined the walls and each was occupied, their operators busy brushing shorn locks into piles beneath the sleek new-wave barber chairs. The male cutters were young Chinese with short and spiky gel haircuts, wearing hipster T-shirts and rip-torn jeans. The female stylists were also young and Chinese, with red or yellow highlights in their chopped hair, their slim bodies wrapped in little denim miniskirts and stretch tank tops that exposed their bellies. Each wore a variation of a wing-style tattoo over her lower back. The colored wings pointed into the crack of their buttocks.

Mona closed her eyes and took several slow, deep breaths, gauging the musty metallic odors, her thumbs nervously working the jade charm in her palm beneath the plastic sheet.

She flipped the coin over, feeling for the symbols on the reverse side.

The women hair stylists had reminded Mona of the *siu jeer,* "young ladies," with whom she'd worked the nightclubs of Hong Kong, and Tsim Sha Tsui. *China City. Volvo Party. Charlie's Club.*

The memories always found their way back to her at the most unexpected moments, the disorienting jolt of seeing herself on her back in the seedy Hong Kong whorehouse, naked, holding back her tears as evil men took turns at her, taking payment in flesh and innocence for the gambling debts her father had owed.

A month like that.

She had been fourteen.

The triad's black-hearted snakes later killed her father anyway. Her mother, a Buddhist, stayed away from the funeral, cursing her *lo gung,* husband, before suffering a fatal heart attack herself.

At fourteen, Mona had found herself alone in the world, and soon discovered how to wield her beauty and her body like Fa Mulan's sword in her hatred of men.

Men were dogs, and she would use that knowledge to her own advantage.

On the reverse of the charm the symbols read *Heaven over Earth.* Evil men block the path of progress. Events turn out badly. Be strong, patient. Gain control.

The stylist lowered the heat dome, announcing, "*Sup fun jung,* ten minutes," as Mona opened her eyes, watching the stylist's tattoo as she sashayed away.

Chameleon

In the mirror, Mona saw the natural beauty of her own face, striking even without a trace of makeup. On the streets, men still stared at her—perfection—inspired by her big deep eyes, her full lips, delicate nose. A look of innocent sorrow to break everyone's heart.

In a Cantonese opera, she would have been the fox, the mesmerizing siren. Classically beautiful, like a young Joan Chen, the actress. Her perfect eyebrows had been tattooed in, and she'd frame her hair around them for a variety of different looks.

A chameleon.

Now Mona was affecting an older face, an older sister, *dai ga jeer.* Fortyish. As a mature businesswoman, she'd be able to sell off the gold and diamonds and all the jewelry she'd acquired.

In the background of the mirror she saw that it continued to rain outside, drops dashing against the street-side windows. It had rained all this week, and most of the last.

Over the passing months, her hair had grown out until it was now shoulder length. When she was in Hawaii, the sun had bleached it, and the last of the highlights had faded to a salt-air brown. Now, she'd brought her hair back to a natural black, the tone of *fot choy* and *mok,* the shade of black moss threads and Chinese ink.

She closed her eyes again, shaking the charm around inside her palm as a Taiwanese ballad faded in over the stereo setup. The music brought her thoughts back to New York City, and Chinatown, and to an old man she'd thought was her ticket out, but who turned out to be a monster in disguise. A Chinatown big shot who'd beat her and raped her.

Her mind drifted to a karaoke bar somewhere far away. At first, all had gone well with the old man whom she'd met first in Kowloon, where hundreds of *siu jeer* sold themselves, trolling for overseas Chinese with the promise of green cards and escape. She'd followed him to New York City, astonished by the energy and madness all around her. She knew her role, overstayed her visa, and disappeared; gone underground.

The old man was thirty years her senior and was married, but he'd provided for her, as his mistress, with a co-op apartment and money for clothes and personal expenses. In return she accompanied him at night, a decoration on his arm that he showed off in the gambling houses and karaoke nightclubs. Men ogled her wherever they went but Uncle Four gave big face to the club owners and didn't bring trouble to their places.

As time went by, he began to accuse Mona of coy and flirtatious behavior in the presence of younger men, causing him loss of face, *mo sai meen*. To an elder man of respect, this was unacceptable. He became abusive and violent, threatening her with deportation, even death, if she ever tried to leave him. As leader of the Hip Chings, his people were everywhere, and she feared she'd never escape.

Jing deng, she cried. It was destiny. Her fate.

He'd beaten and raped her at the slightest whim, loosing an old man's rage against imagined disloyalty and dishonor.

The heating coils hummed along the rim of the dryer dome over the top of her head, baking in the *fot choy,* the blackness.

But she had escaped her destiny, had returned the old bastard's violence with some of her own.

Evil men block the path . . . be strong.

And now she was free.

All regrets are gone. Go forward.

She was ready to move on, take the next step.

Follow the way . . . .

Her hair, clothes, eyes changing. Different tones on her face, lips.

Chameleon.

Safe Deposit

Overseas banks around Chinatown were offering the usual incentives to attract Chinese money. The Far East United Bank rewarded new accounts with a clock radio, preset to receive local Chinese broadcasts. The Regal International Bank countered with an electric rice cooker. Branches of the HKSC presented an array of gift certificates. The China Global Bank boasted a Taiwanese microwave.

Of all the banks in Seattle she'd visited, Mona chose the AAE Bank, situated at the base of a gleaming commercial office tower, halfway between her home and the waterfront. The Asia America Europe bank on Marion, *Ma leon gaai*, offered exactly what she'd needed: a reserved safety deposit box, one of up to five thousand the bank was promoting. The larger the account, the larger the box. With the increase in home-invasions crime, the Chinese bank manager had correctly deduced that there would be a growing demand for secure places to store important documents and valuable items.

For opening an eight-thousand-dollar account, Mona was guaranteed one of the largest units, a green metal container that was twice the size of a shoebox. She'd opened the account over the telephone, through customer service, and now needed only to present the agreed-upon identification and to sign several forms to be assigned the deposit box. She didn't want to spend too much time in the bank, just long enough to access the safety deposit box. She knew she'd turn up on one of the many high-tech surveillance cameras, and desired as low a profile as possible. She understood the value of secrecy.

Just as important, she thought, was that the bank operated branches across three continents, providing safe haven from Asia to Europe, convenient and invaluable for transferring the assets in her account.

The exterior of the Asia America Europe Bank was modern, brass and glass, with huge red block letters AAE mounted above the tall picture windows. Inside, high-tech track lights beamed down from a twenty-foot-high ceiling, illuminating a wall mural depicting an old-time Chinatown montage of street scenes. The business floor was white marble tile, anchoring a corporate presentation that resembled a luxury hotel lobby, with young Chinese in uniform black vests behind a long black stone counter of teller stations. The walls were panels of blond wood, and customer-service agents sat behind matching wood desks in black business suits bearing name tags. Sleek computer stations angled across the desktops.

Mona observed a long queue of customers, heard Asian Muzak floating in the air. The setting felt familiar, comfortable. Welcoming.

She'd worn a conservative black coat over a simple black frock and plain pumps, and a cheap wristwatch just to keep her focused, a prop. The blood-red bangle dangled elegantly off one wrist, her jade charm from a bracelet on the other. She wore no other jewelry except for a plain gold wedding band, another prop, to fend off the men.

Seated at one of the desks, she peered through school-marmish non-prescription glasses, worn for effect, part of the disguise, *jouh hay*. She seemed to be yet another businesswoman, *lo baan leung*, "entrepreneur," boss lady, and yet she appeared elegant in an understated way.

She'd expected, anticipated, the intrusive questions from the managers and the account representatives.

"And in what type of business is Madam invested?"

Marketing and design was her answer.

"Will this be a corporate account? Or a proprietorship?"

Business proprietorship.

"Are you involved with the fashion industry?"

Sometimes.

"The movie industry?"

Sometimes.

She answered the questions in a quiet voice with a small smile, and the young male service agents regarded her with respect, as if she were a *dai ga jeer*, big sister, rather than just a businesswoman.

A clerk brought over some documents for her to sign.

Mona accepted the attention but felt strange knowing her presence was being recorded by the camera system covering the big floor space. She calmed herself, pressing the jade charm inside the soft flesh of her palm.

Again she began with a smile, splaying the identification items onto the blond wood desktop: the Social Security card, the non-driver's license. The young service manager ran his fingers through his gelled-up hair and checked the documents for her signature: *Jing Su Tong*.

Presented with her documents, she saw that she'd

acquired deposit box number 3388, a lucky *fung shui* number, two *yang*s two *yin*s, perfectly balanced to grow and succeed. Her account number was 6818, another auspicious series of numbers: Confident, Wealthy.

Her journey through darkness was turning to light.

The manager moved her along.

Her eyes swept across the bank lobby. No one else seemed to be paying her any unusual attention. Finally, she put away the identification cards, glanced at her watch. Twenty-five minutes had passed.

She was escorted to a secure area where there were private cubicles behind accordion folding doors. She signed for the red cardboard envelope of keys they presented her with.

The big *bo yim seong,* deposit box, was more than large enough to hold her assorted jewelry, the bundled stacks of hundred-dollar bills, the cache of one-ounce gold Panda coins, and the bag of fiery-cut diamonds she would transfer from their hiding place inside the heavy burlap sack of rice. Almost a quarter million dollars' worth of freedom that she'd be entrusting to the care of the AAE Bank. Not for too long, she hoped, before she'd be moving on.

She graciously thanked the manager while returning the empty box, then quickly departed the bank with her keys.

Outside, she felt the weight of the security cameras lift, and she went down a back street knowing she'd return another day soon, in a different guise, to make the deposits that would aid her escape.

The bank account would allow her to transfer cash internationally. As for the gold and diamonds, those she could transport across on a senior citizens' tour bus. North. To *Won Kor Wah*. Vancouver.

Pausing at the street corner, she took a deep breath of the cool morning air, and noted that there were few people around. She still checked to make sure she wasn't being followed, remembering being stalked by homeless men as she passed through Chinatown's adjacent neighborhoods. She didn't see anyone suspicious-looking but she'd felt uneasy for weeks. She wondered if she hadn't been imagining things.

She crossed back to the main street.

The man at the Chinatown market.

She hustled through Pioneer Square, made a quick left on James. Outside the Buddhist Temple, the woman with the man? There seemed to be even fewer people out in the cloudy morning. Something about one of the customers at the bank? The way he'd looked at her? At her brisk pace, she'd soon be home. Was he a black snake? Or just another old horn dog, *hom sup lo*?

I must be losing my mind, she thought, even as she turned for home, to the little basement apartment that held all her hopes.

Changes

Jack awoke to the gray light of the Sea-Tac afternoon, feeling hungry enough to cab up to Chinatown for *congee* and *jow gwai*.

When he checked in at West Precinct Holding Facility, they'd moved Eddie to the Segregation Unit; he'd taken a beatdown and had been terrorized by other prisoners; he was moved for his own protection.

Jack stared at Eddie's swollen black eye and busted lip, and the lumps on the sides of his head. Body bruises no one could see under his clothes. He spoke like he had a wad of cotton in his mouth.

"Those baldy *skinhead* motherfuckers." Eddie spat out the words. "Fuckin' *gwailo* Nazi cocksuckers!"

"Yeah, they got a lot of that out here," Jack commiserated. "Too bad you still got a few days here before you go back into general population."

"No way!" Eddie cursed. "I'm not going back in there."

"They can only hold you in Protective for so long, Eddie," said Jack coolly.

"No fuckin' way," said Eddie as he ran his scraped fingers over his busted eye.

Jack offered quietly, "The only way is if I get a written statement from you. To expedite extradition."

"Extradition?" Eddie winced.

Jack leaned back. "Otherwise, take a seat and get beat. You're just another slab of meat."

"A written statement?"

"Right. A signed confession." Jack rapped his knuckles on the dented metal table. "I take you back to New York. You get a Chinese lawyer, take your chances with a minority jury." Jack saw the light of hope in Eddie's eyes and shoved a pen and pad his way.

"Tell your story as you write it," Jack instructed, "And don't leave out the part where you shoot Koo Jai in the back."

"I get back to New York's Chinatown?" Eddie grimaced.

"Yeah, something like that," Jack answered. "If you cop to the shooting, I can get you out of here, back to New York. Where you'll deal with big-city justice. See?"

There was a pause and Eddie fingered the pen nervously.

"Otherwise," Jack said, drumming his fingers on the tabletop, "you go through Seattle due process, back into general population, and let some white-power prison skinheads fuck you in the ass for two weeks, before you come back to me anyway once the lab matches up the bullet with the gun I found. You know, that gun with your prints all over it? Once we pull your prints off the bag of watches? Along with the vics?"

He could see that Eddie was wavering.

"Come on," Jack pressed, "Your *dailo* said it was you. You and Koo Jai ducked into the alley. Koo had his pockets ripped off and you're the only one who came out of that alley alive. You shot him in the back, then robbed him while he was dying."

Jack took a breath, scowled, and pounded the legal pad.

"That's twenty-five to life, son," he hissed. "So, start talking. Don't waste my time. There's some white boys waiting for your yellow ass back in general."

Eddie, with a look of hate on his mangled face, shook his head and cursed before spitting out clots of words. "We stole these fuckin' watches. The stuff came into some On Yee guy and Koo Jai found out about it. We got into the store, whatever, took the whole shipment. Right out the little window. It was mostly *me*. But it was Koo's hit. *He* set it up. *He* got the best watches. Just like he got the best pussy. Me and the Jung brothers, we knew he didn't want us in the clubhouse. It got in the way of his screwing the sluts up there. Then there was a big stink about the watches. Even the *dailo* came out and made a play. We didn't let on about the watches, but later, Koo gave it up, and we were all fucked. Koo thought if we gave back what was left, it would clear things up. Cool out the loss of face. The stupid ass. The *dailo* scheduled a sit-down but when we hooked up, the big guy started with the shotgun. Then everything got crazy. Fuck!"

He took a deep breath and sat quietly a long time before he finally started writing.

He'd taken a discount Greyhound Coach deal, a series of buses westward to Seattle, the cheapest ticket out of town. Two days felt like four but he knew they wouldn't check for weapons so long as he wasn't crossing any national borders.

He'd carried sixty grand's worth of watches plus what was left of the nine thousand he'd ripped out of Koo's pockets. Fuckin' Koo Jai, pretty-boy faggot *dailo*-wannabe, who'd stepped on his tail once too often.

Deducting for transportation, food, and lodging, life on the lam had left him less than five thousand cash. Trying to get settled, he began selling off the low-end Movados through his *amigos*, Carlos and Jorge. He tried looking for any kind of job he could disappear into but was already tiring of the bad weather.

He'd felt he needed the gun for protection on the road, the only reason he kept it.

He'd shot Koo in self-defense, he insisted, while admitting he'd shot him in the back as Koo was running away in front of him . . .

He blamed everything, the fuck-up with the watches, the OTB shoot-out, on Koo.

The afternoon had brightened by the time the paperwork and the pictures were done. Jack felt a quiet elation. He considered rescheduling his return flight, but realized he would have to forward documents to the NYPD, and to the Tombs, the detention facility outside of Chinatown in New York. Meanwhile, he finally had some time to catch his breath before returning to the motel.

Pike's Market was nearby and he went for black coffee and a snack, and to watch the daylight play over the waters of Elliott Bay. He could see clear across to Harbor Island, past freighters and tugboats and ocean liners. Closer, there were different types of pleasure craft, Sea Rays, and smaller boats. The scene reminded him a little of Sunset Park, where birds and boats docked at the terminal piers. It brought a sense of serenity, the impression that things were going somewhere, had a destination.

Gradually, his thoughts came around to the ORCA Gala, and to Alex. Alexandra. He was anticipating the first and only real opportunity he would have to see her during the entire weekend they'd been in Seattle.

He returned to the motel to press his jacket and pants.

Syuhn Ferry

She'd always liked being near water, her element, and her frequent walks to the bay familiarized her with the piers and the boats plying their way in different directions.

The Chinatown travel agency had been very helpful; she'd booked a ferry excursion with an overnight stay to tour the northern city of Victoria, but more important, to spend a few hours in the Chinese communities there. She was reminded of the Queen Victoria landmarks she'd seen in Hong Kong.

The ferry would depart in the early morning, and meals were not included. She'd gone to Mon Chang Supermarket the night before and purchased a plastic container of *cha siew*, roast pork, and bags of rice crackers and *chun pui mui,* preserved plums.

The voyage would be a three-hour cruise each way, through Puget Sound and the northern straits. The weather was cool, foggy, and she layered her clothing under a black rain jacket, carrying only the big red plastic bag with the Mon Chang logo.

The other Asians aboard were Japanese and Korean tourist families out for a day trip.

The ferry boat had several decks and Mona had gone to the top, pausing at the rail to watch the boat leave the dock. As the boat churned into the bay a sudden gust of wind snatched the Mon Chang Supermarket's plastic bag from her grasp, carrying it toward the water. She could only watch as the wind dashed the red bag of snacks into the riptides.

In her distress, she clutched the charm in her fist, and swallowed a breath. The red jade bangle turned cold on her wrist, its chill like a warning.

Follow the flow, the charm advised, test the waters.

She dragged her thumbnail across its jade surface again.

Faith avoids disaster.

As the ferry cut its way into Puget Sound, she kept her focus on the red plastic bag, watching it swirl and bob, the weight inside of the *cha siew*, roast pork, and the *chun pui mui* keeping it in the water, while the sealed bag of rice crackers kept it afloat.

The flow washed the red bag onto the shore near a park and a pier leading to a group of big red umbrellas she recognized as part of the sundeck of the Spa Garden.

The ferry gained speed, signaling with a blast of its horn.

She took a breath and sat on a bench by the rail, watching the red bag disappear into the distance, along with the big red umbrellas and the small patch of beachfront park. How blessed, she mused, the wind and water giving me direction.

Her view slowly encompassed mountains crowned by a blue haze, and bald eagles swooping past old forts and lighthouses. She'd lost her appetite and decided to eat after they reached Victoria. Chinese food, she figured, in Chinatown. There were no whales to be seen but the scenic landscapes soothed her.

When they arrived at the Inner Harbor, the weather had cleared considerably. The beautiful bay was sparkling, and she checked into the nearby James Bay Inn. Shortly after, she toured the streets en route to Chinatown, and passed under a Gate of Harmonious Interest. She felt another layer of dread lift. This Chinatown was old, but not very far from the ones she'd visited in Vancouver.

The ferry would return her to *Say nga touh*, Seattle, the next afternoon.

Red King

He shuffled the deck and deftly fanned the cards out. The articulation had become second nature. He packed the deck, then cut it into halves, folded them back together.

Gee Sin shifted the cell phone, waited for the connection to clear. The line had experienced interference recently. He flipped out a card, replacing it in the deck. Flipping the cards open-faced had been harder to master, having as much to do with the thumb and finger as with wrist and forearm.

He flipped up a pair of jacks.

Jacks in the morning, the king takes warning.

Outside his picture window, the clouds spread over Victoria Harbour under a shrimp-gray sky. He swallowed a Vicodin, chasing it with a shot of brandy, neat. The splash of cold water that followed chilled the fire in his throat. He knew the painkiller would make a beeline to his brain.

It was Tsai's voice on the international connection to New York, giving Gee Sin the call he knew would come. Tsai, still a 432, Gee Sin evaluated, but up and coming.

Paper Fan saw the gloomy expanse of the Wan Chai waterfront, the Mid-Levels, Mongkok, fading into the soupy mist. He held the cell phone to his left ear with his shoulder, shuffled the deck again, and spread the cards out on the countertop.

"This comes to us," Tsai said, "from one of our *sister* Grass Sandals."

There was a short burst of static over the line. Gee Sin knew some of the local chapters had recruited women into their operations.

"A woman made a donation to a temple," Tsai continued, "in *Say nga touh*."

Gee Sin understood that he meant Seattle, and asked, "Don't women make donations all the time?"

"Yes, but not in *gold*," emphasized Tsai. "They don't usually donate gold coins."

"A coin?" Gee Sin remembered the stolen one-ounce Pandas. "What make of coin?"

"A gold Panda." Tsai paused. "She wasn't sure what size."

"But why donate a gold coin?" Gee Sin felt the pulling drifting sensation of the Vicodin. There was more breakup, *clicking* on the line.

"It's an old way of thinking," said Tsai. "From when our countrymen were refugees, during *jo non*, fleeing from the Japanese. Our *hingdaai*, brothers, converted all their paper money to gold. Because metal doesn't burn like paper does, and gold doesn't lose its value like government currency."

Gee Sin gave this a moment, then asked, "Was this an older woman, then?"

"No, she fit the general profile. Thirties to forties, short to average height."

"What else?" asked Gee Sin, the brandy rushing through his blood now.

"The monk said she prayed briefly and left."

"Is that strange?" He caressed the deck of cards, his vision starting to blur.

"Well, it was after the Lantern Festival. Lots of people in and out of the temple. Our female *cho hai* there reported that the sister monk remembered that the woman didn't sign the log-in book."

They waited through a moment of crackling noise.

Tsai continued, "She said the woman was dressed all in black, and reminded her of a movie star in a magazine."

"You have people in place?" Gee Sin's words began to slur.

"We're watching the temple," Tsai said crisply, "with help from local 49s, Hip Ching *say gow jai*, fighters."

"Where are you now?" Gee Sin heard himself asking.

"I'm preparing to go to the airport. JFK."

Gee Sin didn't approve of using the 49s, but advised, "Call me when you get to *Say nga touh*." He hung up, and put the cell phone down.

The deck of cards beckoned him as a feeling of goodness and compassion washed over him. He squeezed the deck and smoothly flipped out the top three cards.

A King of Hearts.

A Queen of Spades.

A King of Diamonds.

He put the deck down. A black, *hak,* queen, trapped between a pair of blood-red kings.

Soon, Gee Sin the Paper Fan anticipated, the trail ends.

Fot Mong, Nightmare

Mona felt groggy, looking up as if in a daze, snug beneath a shiny black covering, a blanket. She was observing a candlelit ceremony of some kind, two men in robes, Buddhist-like, in front of an altar. One man wore a red sash, the other a green headband. The shadowy air was thick with incense. Chanting? But *not* Buddhist.

The man who was the Incense Master wore a grass sandal on his left foot and was exchanging hand signals with the gathering of new recruits.

She was almost swept away by a wave of dizziness.

She'd thought the recruits were dogs at first, obediently seated on their haunches. The murmuring sound cut abruptly to silence and she soon realized these were men on their knees, sitting back on their heels. Their faces were flickering images in the candlelight, glimpses of an ancient ritual. They were reciting an oath.

I shall not betray my brethren . . .

Angling for a better view, she discovered she was bound onto a black mattress, spread-eagled and naked under the covering. Like a sacrificial lamb.

I shall not betray. The penalty is death. The oaths declined to murmurs again.

Then the Incense Master held up a Ming Dynasty–type dagger, and the recruits turned their attention to her on the mattress. She saw lines of leering lecherous men, evil *hock sear wui,* snakeheads, rising up from their crouched postures.

They formed a long line as, to her shock, the black satin sheet that was covering her was slowly pulled away, exposing all of her in the dim shadowy light. With lolling, dripping tongues, the men resembled dogs again. Triad mongrels.

She struggled against the ties that bound her, helpless. It only excited the men more. She screamed as the first group of men surrounded her, screamed as the first engorged erection penetrated her.

Yelling, she'd jerked herself awake. She was sitting upright in her own bed, her heart pounding even in the reassuring quiet of her basement apartment. She caught her breath trying to shake the *fot mong,* nightmare, from her head, clutching the jade charm in her fist.

Beware, it warned, beware.

She'd already transferred half of her bank account to the Vancouver branch of the AAE bank. She'd be able to transport the remaining gold and diamonds traveling overland by bus, or else by sea, on a ferry.

Gradually, her spirit calmed, but she could not find sleep, wondering how she could advance her plans.

Thunder over Water floated to the surface of the charm, tingling at her fingertips.

Find direction, it urged, make haste to go.

Jun bay, prepare.

She took the razor blade from the travel sewing kit and slit open the edge where the padded lining met the hem of the jacket, a cheap black barn jacket she'd bought at the Ming Wah Mall. All the old Chinese wore the same drab discount items from the Chinese mall stores and she wanted to blend into the mix when the time came.

She spread the seam open with her fingers, popping the thread work until the opening was more than the width of her hand.

She grabbed a plastic bag from the makeshift kitchenette, a clear Ziploc bag that was large enough to hold a magazine. She neatly inserted bank documents, a paper-clipped stack of eight one-hundred-dollar bills, and a mini zip-bag containing six diamonds wrapped in wax paper. She added the little red envelope with the key to the safe deposit box, and the Social Security card identifying her as Jing Su Tong.

Pressing the air out, she zipped the plastic bag and slipped it beneath the lining of the jacket. She inserted her hand and spread the plastic flat, patting it into place. From the sewing kit, she got a needle and ran six loose loops of thread and closed the edge at lining and hem. It will be easier to open when the time comes, she thought, remembering *Make haste to go.*

She kept the Seattle non-driver's license in her pocket, the photo ID describing her as Tong J. Su: 118 pounds. Twenty-eight years old. She'd memorized the numbers 2, 11, 8: all auspicious.

At the foot of her bed, the black rubber "Prago" bag was a knockoff, a zippered shoulder bag big enough to hold travel necessities, and then some. She'd also found it at Ming Wah, where cheap copies of the world's best designs were available. Into the shoulder bag she tossed a Chinese newspaper, a senior citizen's discount bus voucher, a souvenir Chinatown letter opener. She clipped the travel brochures from Trans World Asia together, tossing them in. She'd made advance arrangements for Vancouver, a week's stay at the Budget Hotel near Chinatown. She'd also booked a tour, a bus shuttle from Victoria to Vancouver.

Beware, beware.

She caressed the red bangle with her thumb, urging forth luck and courage.

She placed eight gold Panda coins into the inside zipper-pouch of the black carry-all. In her pants pocket was a thousand dollars in folded hundred-dollar bills. She'd still need heaven's help, she knew, but at least the numbers were on her side.

A huge Chinese crowd thronged the lobby of the Westin, milling and mixing its way toward the music inside the ballroom. The gourmet-dinner portion of the event had concluded, the awards had already been presented, and the liquor was flowing freely.

Jack straightened his jacket and joined the shuffling, swaying procession heading toward the bright lights and raucous laughter. Inside the cavernous ballroom, a Filipino rock band was banging out "La Bamba." The crowd near the stage bopped and hopped to the beat. Young Chinese-American ORCA interns were letting off corporate steam as Jack scanned the crowd for Alex. Lots of men in tuxedoes and old money all around, thought Jack.

All the sophisticated ladies wore jazzy gowns and the scene was loud, jamming, and everything looked fabulous. Jack made his way toward the stage. More women, shiny dresses, glittering jewelry, and coiffed hair. A flute of champagne in every delicate hand.

He heard quick exchanges of repartee everywhere. Everyone looked rich and carefree.

Alex suddenly emerged from a group of designer tuxedoes and shimmering outfits. She was radiant in a gold dress and heels, with all the fine accessories, reveling in her moment. She came toward him with a long lingering smile, followed it with a kiss on his cheek.

"*Finally,*" she said. "Glad you could make it."

The group of CADS and ORCAs noticed Jack, and his familiarity with Alex.

"Ladies' room calling," she said, smiling. "I'll be right back. Go ahead and mingle."

"Sure," Jack said, scanning the hundreds of exquisitely dressed Chinese. He watched her walk away, a gold sheath swaying to the music, until she disappeared into the masses. He wasn't the mingling type, he thought.

One of the CADS greeted him with, "You must be the lawman Alexandra told us about." Another lawyer-type turned and said, "Why don't you regale us with some of your adventures?"

Jack was momentarily speechless, holding his thoughts but displaying a smile on his face. Regale? he mused. I'm here to entertain you? He bit down inside the frozen smile. Adventures? Murder and horrific brutality were *adventures*? He wondered if it was too soon to dislike them, and decided to wait until Alex returned.

Abruptly, ADA Bang Sing stepped from the group and came to Jack's social rescue.

"Detective," Sing said, "I hate to talk shop but can I have a word?"

"Sure," Jack answered, gratefully. "Excuse us, gentlemen."

They stepped away, joining another crowd beside one of the mobile bars.

"Don't mind them," Sing explained. "They get a little obnoxious after a few drinks." He paused, then grinned. "You know how lawyers are."

"Yeah, right," Jack said, smiling. "But thanks anyway. Anything new with the Johnny Wong case?"

"No," Sing replied. "He's still cooling at Rikers. But he's getting more calls from Hong Kong."

"He's allowed calls?" puzzled Jack.

"E-mails," Sing said.

"About what?"

Bang Sing shrugged. "That's all I know."

Jack took a breath, saw the group of CADS from the distance. They were partying hearty to the booming beat, and oddly enough, he felt happy for them. They deserved it. For their time and commitment to righteous causes. Party on, by any means necessary.

At the bar, they pounded beers. "Thanks again," Jack repeated, wondering now about Sing's relationship to Alex. Relationship?

"Sure thing," Bang Sing toasted, "sure thing."

It seemed as if the crowd parted for Alex as she returned, a vision more lovely than Jack had recalled. She took him by the hand, led him away from ADA Sing and the crowded floor.

They lit up cigarettes near a side exit, refreshed by the cool night air.

"This is great," Jack said. "But for the record, I did try to call you last night."

"Last night?" Alex sounded puzzled.

"It was late," Jack continued. "Some *man* answered."

"Man? *Who*?" she challenged.

"Don't know," Jack demurred, "didn't ask."

"Well, the bunch of us went room-hopping," Alex recalled. "Drinking nightcaps. Why didn't you leave me a message?"

"It was late. I didn't want to interrupt." Jack crushed out his cigarette.

"Interrupt?" she said skeptically. "Interrupt *what*?" She paused. "Were you annoyed?" Another pause as she finished her cigarette. "Wait . . . you weren't jealous, were you?"

"Jealous?" Jack laughed, "*Me*? Why would I be jealous?"

Alex smiled a knowing smile, shook her head at him. "*Right.* Who'd be hitting on me anyway, right? The lady's got baggage, going through a divorce, has a kid, drinks too much . . ."

"I didn't mean that," said Jack defensively. "I never said *that*."

Alex took his hand again. "Come on, let's go," she said quietly.

"Where?" he asked as he looked back toward the ballroom. "You've got music, alcohol, right in there."

"I've had enough drinking and dancing for a weekend," she offered. "Plus I owe you a rain check. From New York."

"Yeah," Jack remembered. "Espresso, with sambuca."

"You've got a good memory," he heard her say. "Then again, you're a cop."

He put out his cigarette, said, "Okay, sure," and followed her back through the crowd.

In the Mood for Love

Her suite was small but featured two single beds and some countertop space that also served as TV stand and coffee table.

"Weren't you rooming with someone?" Jack asked as Alex prepped the coffeemaker. She was a bit tipsy in her heels, and he noticed the bottle of sambuca had already been opened.

"Joann left already," she answered. "She had an eleven o'clock flight." She dimmed the light from the table lamps.

"Red-eye back to New York, huh?"

"Right." She poured shots of the sambuca liqueur.

Jack could smell the coffee brewing, then the fragrance of herbal shampoo, or body spray, as Alex nudged up beside him, high heels off now, in her bare feet.

"So, how was your weekend?" she asked, lighting a cigarette.

"You wouldn't believe it." He wanted badly to tell her, to brag a little, but knew better. She helped him out of his jacket, draping it over the lone chair.

"Try me," she challenged.

"Let's just say I caught a bad guy." He grinned.

"Always the good cop, huh?" she quipped, taking a sip of the liqueur. She clicked on the bedside radio to a bluesy saxophone tune, then dialed down the volume to low.

He noticed a wood-and-brass plaque with her name on it and an inscribed crystal bowl on her night table.

"Congratulations," he said admiringly.

"Thanks," she replied with a big smile. "Coffee's almost ready."

He resisted the urge to hug her, to taste the sweetness of the sambuca that glistened on her lips.

"What?" she said as she noticed his stare. "Is there something on my face?"

"No, it just feels good to look at you."

"You drunk or something?" she teased.

"Nowhere near as drunk as *you* are," he teased back.

"Oh yeah?" She poured a little more liqueur over the coffee in the little Styrofoam cups and took a sip. "Here you go," she said, abruptly planting a soft kiss on his lips, the taste of espresso trailing her smoky breath.

He took a steamy sip of the mixture.

"You know this will keep you up," he warned.

"Exactly," she grinned. "My final night in Seattle. I want to make it last."

They savored the aroma, then rested their cups on the countertop. She closed her eyes and slowly rolled her neck. He massaged her taut shoulders, which brought a deep sigh from her. He smelled a musky scent emanating from her.

Alex turned and looped her arms over his shoulders, leaning into his body. Jack pulled her even closer, his hands sliding to her hips. They found themselves drifting to the slow grind of saxophone blues, and he assumed that the electricity dancing between their bodies came from the shuffling friction of their feet along the carpet.

He could see questions in her eyes, even in the dim shadowy light.

It started with a series of light, little kisses, with his lips lingering on hers, then pulling back slightly, savoring it. He was captivated by the scent of her skin, the warm licorice exhalation of her breath. More kisses were exchanged between searching looks, questions unanswered in the fleeting moments.

"Unzip me," she said softly, and he tugged the zipper down smoothly to the small of her back. She shrugged her shoulders and twisted against him until the gold dress fell away to reveal skimpy gold satin lingerie.

He took a breath before kissing her hard on the fleshy part of her throat. She shuddered, and reached for his belt buckle just as his cell phone vibrated. A buzz kill.

His first thought was to ignore the call. Surely it could wait, damnit. But after the second vibration he wondered who might be calling at this hour, here in Seattle. He thought it might be Detective Nicoll, or SPD, something to do with Eddie Ng in custody. A quick update? His curiosity got the better of him and he shot Alex a sheepish look before backing away to take the call.

He never took his eyes off her until his cell-phone screen lit up the frown across his face. It was Captain Marino, transferring a trans–Atlantic call through bursts of static interference. Something to do with the northern lights.

The international call had been patched through via the 0-Five, vetted and approved, Jack guessed, by Captain Marino himself. The Royal Hong Kong Police was partnering with INTERPOL, he heard through the static.

Jack recalled different law enforcement agencies as he waited through the introduction. INTERPOL was shorthand for the International Criminal Police Organization, headquartered in Lyon, France. It consisted of more than a hundred member nations and dealt with international crime through local law enforcement. Its focus included watching for lost or stolen passports and locating fugitives from justice.

A Red Notice was INTERPOL's highest level of alert, an arrest warrant that circulated worldwide.

The RHKP's voice was typically Chinese-British, formal and to the point: "A fugitive who is a top member of an unlawful secret society may have arrived in the United States, at Seattle. His name is not important, as he travels under an alias anyway. He is sixty-three years old, a number 415 Paper Fan rank, in the second tier of command of the *Hung Huen,* Red Circle triad, a criminal organization."

Jack quickly recalled what he knew about triads, their ranks, their history. He could hear the echo of Lucky's words, rapping about the tongs. Triads were Chinese secret societies, benevolent brotherhoods that went back through the centuries. Mostly now they were criminal gangs operating out of Hong Kong and China, gangs that had fingers in everything from China White heroin to human trafficking. Everything from knockoff handbags to money fraud, not to mention gambling, gang protection and prostitution, muscle mayhem and murder.

As for how the ranks were set up, Jack knew it all started at the top with the Dragon Head, the *loong tauh.* Lucky had demonstrated some secret hand signals once. Beneath the

Dragon were several officers: a planner, *consigliere*, called Paper Fan. An enforcer known as a Red Pole. Couriers, like liaisons, were Grass Sandals. Then there were other ranks Jack wasn't sure of. Incense Master. Vanguard. The stuff of folklore and Chinese legends.

The sambuca was working against his mental clarity now. He felt the thirst for alcohol even though he knew hot tea would be better.

"Hocus-pocus, "Lucky had said, *ho-cuss poke us*. "Fuck *dat*, kid. Me and the boyz are blood-in by deed, understand? We ain't lighting candles and reciting shit, and jumping through smoke. We ain't pledging to nothing but the dollars. Kill the chicken, drink the blood? Get the fuck outta here. Each of my boyz came in and did the *deed*, you know it? This ain't no fuckin Boy Scouts, okay? China White? Yeah, their H is hot, but we ain't jumping through no hoops for it. Membership? We like the money *maker*, not the money *taker*. We don't pay dues, we *collect* dues."

Big statements from Lucky, thought Jack. Comatose at Downtown now.

There were three hundred thousand triad members in Hong Kong. Not counting the members across the waters, in China and Taiwan.

The RHKP's voice continued after a quick breath. Jack wondered if he was being read a prepared statement.

"Paper Fan faces numerous warrants for currency and credit card fraud, money laundering, human trafficking, child pornography, prostitution, and copyright piracy."

Jack listened patiently, feeling his lips going dry.

"Billions of dollars of theft. He is suspected of

191

involvement in three homicides in three different countries. While he is highly insulated in Hong Kong, and well protected in Canada, he avoids Amsterdam, where he is vulnerable to drug charges. He travels infrequently but we believe he can be taken in the United States. Therefore the Red Notice to your headquarters. As always, we are grateful for your cooperation."

Jack glanced at Alex, who had slipped on a robe, and was sipping sambuca again.

"Why Seattle?" Jack asked.

"The triad believes there's a woman there who they want badly."

A woman?

"A woman who stole something from them. A woman they believe killed someone in your precinct, in Chinatown New York."

Mona, Jack knew immediately. Here in Seattle? How much "destiny" could he take?

"What do you have on her?" he asked.

"They believe she visited a temple."

"Temple?"

"And we have an address. It's on South King Street"

"What about Paper Fan?" Jack redirected.

"Find the woman, and you'll find him."

Thanks, thought Jack, another shot in the dark.

In the dim light he could see Alex giving him the look, asking, What's up? They were losing the moment, had lost the moment, passion dissolved into the coffee and the background music.

"And she's *where?*" Jack asked.

"She's in south Seattle, somewhere in the five-mile area of Chinatown. We don't know where exactly. Yet."

Jack rubbed his temple, trying to clear his head.

"I will keep you posted," the RHKP voice promised, "since we have a direct connection now."

"Ten-four that," Jack acknowledged, making a note of the address.

"The Red Notice covers everything."

"Ten-four that," Jack repeated, hanging up as Alex nuzzled into him. "I'm sorry," he apologized to Alex, and briefly explained the new developments.

When she heard "human trafficking," she said, "I'm going with you."

He considered the situation as she changed into a sweater and jeans. Because the scent of Alex still lingered, and against his better judgment, he would allow her to come along. It may come to nothing, he thought.

It was past 1 AM as Jack passed the updated INTERPOL information into Detective Nicoll's voice mail.

"We need to get to South King," Jack said.

Alex borrowed a car from a member of the local ORCA chapter and they got directions from the hotel concierge. They drove toward the waterfront until they found the temple on South King at the edge of Chinatown. The street was deserted during the graveyard hours, but in the yellow light of streetlamps they could make out the signage above a storefront. The words PURE LIFE WORLD TEMPLE ran across the front, which bore a pagoda motif.

The temple was closed but Jack observed a dark sedan parked farther down the empty street. It had California plates, and he associated that with San Francisco. He saw two occupants, male, as he drove past. And there was a big dent on the rear fender.

"Let's circle the block," he said, wheeling the car right around the corner.

They came around again, well behind the parked sedan this time. Jack pulled in half a block away and killed the headlights. Two men, at this hour? He wondered if they had noticed him, wondered if it had been wise to allow Alex to tag along.

"Stay put," he told her. "I'm going to have a look."

"Careful," she said quietly, unable to conceal her concern.

"Yeah, sure," he said as he exited the car. Could be anything, he told himself, could be nothing. Play it by the book.

Alex watched as Jack went down the dark street. He was still three car lengths away when a Chinese man wearing wire-frame eyeglasses stepped out of the passenger side and walked away from Jack. The man, who was slightly built, took off his glasses and pocketed them as Jack neared the driver's side.

Jack reached into his pocket, palming his detective's gold shield. Could be nothing, he thought again. He leaned toward the car and flashed the badge as the driver powered down his window.

"*Aww, chaai lo ah?*" the thick Chinese face said, smiling. A cop, huh?

Cantonese, Jack recognized, his eyes darting momentarily toward the man who'd left the sedan, who'd thrown a look back over his shoulder.

"*Jouh matyeh a?*" Jack asked the driver. "What's up?"

"*Mo yeh,* nothing much, *ah sir,*" the driver answered with sarcasm in his voice.

The second man stopped walking and turned toward Jack. His hands went into his jacket pockets. Let me see your hands, Jack was thinking, his attention divided. The slim man muttered something under his breath; it sounded like *dew nei louh mou.* Fuck you, motherfucker.

Suddenly, the driver threw the car door open, knocking Jack backward.

The second man stepped toward Jack as the driver sprang from the car. He was tall and rangy, maybe six foot two.

Alex watched with astonishment when the shorter man reached back and flung something that struck Jack with great force. Reflexively, he clutched at his ribs, and was distracted long enough for the big man to whip out a pair of nunchakus.

To Alex it was like a chop-socky sequence in a bad kung-fu movie.

The smaller man took two quick-bounding steps and then threw a high kick at Jack's head. Jack blocked the kick with a *bow arm,* deflecting it with his elbow, but the contact threw him off balance. The big man flailed wildly with the metal nunchakus and caught Jack across the shoulder, then slammed him a second time before he could pull his service revolver. The second man pulled a knife from his waist as Jack fell to the pavement.

Jack could hear Alex screaming as the smaller man lunged at him with the thick blade. Snapping a straight kick upward into the man's knee, Jack rolled instinctively just as

195

the iron nunchakus slammed into the asphalt near his head. He pulled his Colt Special and aimed it, but the knife man lashed out a front kick that sent the gun clattering across the street.

Alex's screaming got louder, closer.

"Jouh!" he heard the big man yell. "Split!" The goon hadn't figured on assaulting a woman.

Struggling to his feet, Jack saw Alex dashing his way as the big man started up the sedan.

"Stay back!" Jack yelled, but Alex had already flashed past him, still screaming like a madwoman.

The knife man cursed and dove into the passenger side as the car screeched away.

Jack retrieved his Colt, watching the sedan disappear around the corner and into the black night. Alex came back to him, her face flushed and gasping for air. He caught his breath, patting his ribs and left side. Something had struck him and was embedded in the thick folds of his jacket. When he worked it loose he saw it was a razor-sharp five-pointed *shuriken*, a throwing star, a weapon that ninja assassins used centuries earlier. It had pierced his bunched-up garments but had barely broken his skin.

"What the hell was that all about?" Alex asked incredulously.

"They were waiting for someone," Jack answered, pocketing the *shuriken*, "and it sure wasn't Buddha."

The message he left with Nicoll sounded like a telegram: "Two AM, Got call from INTERPOL. Went to South King, got into a fight. Two men, Chinese. Something to do with a triad." Pause. "Or a tong. There's another person of interest, who may be a suspect. A woman. Keep in touch."

Jack brought Alex back to his airport motel room, where she applied ice packs to the swollen welts that ran across his left shoulder. He could tell she was embarrassed by the economy room, comparing it to hers at the Westin.

She noticed old scars on his chest and arms, and remembered visiting him in the hospital after he'd been shot while investigating the murder of the food delivery boy.

Meanwhile the big man with the iron nunchakus had reminded Jack of Golo, the tall Hip Ching enforcer, and the vicious fight they'd had in Brooklyn's Chinatown. They'd wounded each other then, but Jack had since left Golo very dead on a San Francisco rooftop. Now Jack was again chasing the same woman who, in his mind's eye, was just a fleeting image disappearing behind a rooftop door as he sent two hollow-point bullets after her.

The triad information from INTERPOL made Jack think of the old men of the Hip Ching Benevolent Association back in New York; they'd played dumb about their murdered boss, offering up the Fukienese newcomers as bait.

Jack felt that the fight and flight on South King had the stink of the Hip Chings around it. It'd been their business from the start and they were finishing it now. The Paper Fan was connected to the Hip Chings somehow, and Jack heard the echo of the RHKP's voice: Find the woman, you'll find him.

It was almost 3 AM when he and Alex delved back into the Seattle directories. They sought addresses for anything Hip Ching: cultural organizations, benevolent societies, trade associations, credit unions, fraternal and village societies, immigrant self-help services.

Outside the motel window the night sky had opened up to pounding sheets of rain.

Within an hour they'd narrowed it down to an address in Chinatown that housed three Hip Ching-affiliated organizations. Three, a magic Chinese number, Jack knew.

Alex was wide-eyed, wired.

The adrenaline and the espresso-and-liqueur mixture had juiced them up, and they went to the car for the drive back to Chinatown.

One False Move

He'd had a fitful sleep on the bed of the convertible couch in the back office of the Benevolent Association. He was concerned about not leaving a trace of his stay in *Say nga touh*, and his throbbing knee hadn't responded to the hot towel wrap.

Tsai grimaced as he rubbed the pungent brown *deet da jow* along the outside of his left knee, where the Chinese *chaai lo* cop had kicked him. The liniment bit at his nostrils. I should have gone for the face, Tsai thought, closing his eyes as he put more pressure into the rub. It would have had a greater impact. He'd played it safe, had chosen to go for the torso, the bigger target, instead of the head, aiming the *shuriken* into the cop's gut.

Tsai measured his breathing, twisted his face away from the smell of the *deet da jow*. He imagined the big 49 fighter flailing with his metal nunchakus. A big lug, lacking in training. They'd let the cop off lightly. And women were bad luck, he cursed, rubbing anger into the pain around his knee.

They'd have to be more discreet about the temple now.

Women Hold Up Half the Sky

The call from the female Grass Sandal assuaged Tsai's pain, although he still felt bad luck in the air. She'd been ambitious and had discovered another connection to the missing woman, Mona.

This discovery had come about precisely because she was a woman and undoubtedly would garner her some attention from the triad's national ranks.

In the privacy of the front office, Tsai rested his leg on the coffee table, looked out over Elliott Bay, and listened to her report.

"She's found a woman doctor," the Grass Sandal said.

Tsai assumed she meant a female doctor.

"An ob-gyn," she added for detail, "a woman's doctor."

The clarification was sharp; of course he hadn't considered it. *A woman's doctor.*

Acting on a hunch, the female 432 had guessed that a woman of Mona's experience would seek out a gynecologist and, because she was Chinese, would probably prefer a female doctor. Checking the local listings for women's medical services around the Chinatown area, she had narrowed the choices down to two female doctor: an Indian and a Vietnamese-Chinese.

The Indian doctor required medical insurance, but the Vietnamese occasionally accepted cash. From new patients, all that was required was a photo ID and a mailing address where she could send follow-up reports.

The female 432 had visited the Vietnamese doctor, had filled in the required information in the New Patient sign-in log, and had prepaid with cash. After the exam, she used the bathroom while the doctor prepared for her next patient. On the way out, she pilfered the log-in ledger, which contained the addresses of the year's new patients. One in particular stood out.

A Chinese woman had paid cash, and had given an address on James Street.

Tsai commended the Grass Sandal's smart work, and formally thanked her for her diligence and ingenuity. He made a note of the address and then hung up.

The address was not far from Chinatown.

Dew keuih, Tsai muttered as he rubbed in the rest of the liniment, fuck her.

Considering how he would approach Mona, he scanned the shelves of the association office; they were filled with stacks of Chinese newspapers and magazines, assorted health-care and census forms.

The Benevolent Association had sponsored several Chinese-speaking census takers as part of a community outreach program. They'd registered several dozen American-born Chinese but knew that thousands of Chinese illegals would never respond.

But it was good public relations. Face.

He grabbed a clipboard from the desk and slipped an artist's likeness of Mona under the clip. He covered it with a stack of census forms. After wiping clear his wire-frame glasses, he patted his aching knee and hoped the smell of the liniment would be less noticeable with his pants on.

He grimaced as he limped out of the office in the direction of James Street.

Mourning Rain

The Hip Ching address was on Jackson Street, not far from Hing Hay Park in the old section of Chinatown. The building was dark, a six-story hulk that featured a pagoda facade above two large lion dog statues guarding the front door.

Jack and Alex sat in the car, a block away, watching the pouring rain usher in the Seattle dawn. No one appeared, and when it got light enough, Jack drove the car around a ten-block radius, checking out the area. The streets were still deserted. But Jack soon came to an alleyway off Weller, where he found what he was hoping for. The dark sedan that had carried the two men he'd fought with was parked halfway on the sidewalk. He saw the California plates clearly. Jack parked opposite the mouth of the narrow alley where he had a good view of the intersection as well. He walked across and checked out the dent on the rear fender. No doubt. When he came back to the car Alex rested her head against his good shoulder and they waited.

Jack knew Mona was involved in the killing of Uncle Four in New York, and that the elderly Hip Ching leader was connected to Paper Fan and the triad. She'd taken something, something important enough for them to jump into the wind after her. This was what it was all about.

Instinctively, he felt the woman was close at hand.

Alex ran into Chinatown and bought *baos, lor bok go,* lo

mein, and four cups of black Chinese coffee, bound to keep them hyper. More people appeared on the streets: Chinatown folks going about their morning routines, students heading for school, office workers going to day jobs.

Many men walked past the car but none of them looked like the men from the temple fight.

By the time they dumped the food cartons the rain had stopped.

Sense Us

Wearing the black coat over the black frock, the business pumps, and the drugstore eyeglasses, Mona was ready for the necessary transactions at the AAE Bank, the final actions before she'd *fey*, jump back into the wind.

The morning was camouflage gray but she noticed him the moment she stepped out of the house; a slightly built bespectacled Chinese man who looked a little too old to be a student, carrying a pen and a clipboard that had the Chinese characters for CENSUS marked across the back.

He saw her at the same moment, pausing to check something on the clipboard. He approached her as she started to walk away.

"*Nay ho?*" he began politely in Cantonese, How are you?, readying his pen at the clipboard. "I'm conducting a residential survey for the census. May I ask you a few questions?"

"I'm sorry," she replied quickly. "I'm only visiting. I'm not from here."

"I see," the man said easily, noticing a resident exiting an adjacent home. He gave her a lingering glance, nodding his thanks before heading toward the other house.

She noticed that he walked with a slight limp.

From a block away she looked back over her shoulder and saw the man engaged in a conversation with a Filipino. He checked his watch and didn't seem to be looking in her direction.

Two blocks away she decided to take a different route, passing through the Won Chang Mall, just to be on the safe side.

Back on James Street, the man watched as Mona quickly disappeared around a corner, a thin smile twisting up his mouth. No need to follow for now, Tsai thought. Her height and hair could be misleading, he knew, recalling her features as compared to the likeness on his clipboard. The eyeglasses, also, were a distraction. He hadn't been able to get a good look without staring at her. She'd appeared nervous and he hadn't wanted to spook her. But what got his attention was the flash of the gold bracelet on her wrist, and the jade charm dangling off it; a round white tablet covered with faint veins of gray. She wears the *bot kwa* on her wrist, the Taoist etchings clear to see. Just the way the limo driver Johnny Wong had described from his jail cell.

Now that he was sure she was the one, he needed only to wait for the arrival of Paper Fan, knowing the leader would want to be in on the snatch. They planned to take her to a Hip Ching property on Harbor Island, where gang-rape for videotape awaited her, before being taken back to Hong Kong, where they would force her to whore-off what she had stolen.

Shadows in Seattle

It was mid-afternoon and Alex spotted them first, the two men from the temple fight. They came down the alleyway wearing dark rain jackets, the big man lumbering along, and the slight man walking with a hitch in his gait. I should have snapped his knee, Jack thought with regret.

The men slipped into the sedan and waited as windshield wipers cleared their view.

Jack knew he could bust them for assault but he would have to call in the SPD and he realized there was more at stake. He chose to let the bad kharma ride. After a few minutes, a gray minivan rolled up to the intersection and pulled in at the curb.

The sedan flashed its headlights twice.

Things stayed that way until the sedan pulled off the sidewalk and slowly came out of the alley. The minivan fell in behind.

Jack keyed the ignition, gave them a block's distance before he started tailing them. They came to a busy avenue and mixed in with afternoon traffic, with Jack still several cars back. After a ten-minute drive, a short distance, they reached James Street. The sedan and minivan pulled over as Jack passed them and circled, figuring he'd double back and wind up watching them from behind.

The street was quiet when Jack pulled back into James Street.

It started to rain again as everyone waited.

Blind Faith

Mona knew that a brisk walk would bring her to the water-front in twenty minutes. Even in the light rain, it would take her no more than twenty-five minutes. She'd abandon the tour bus plan and take the ferry, right now.

She'd chosen the running sneakers she'd always worn with her jogging outfit from the Spa Garden. Her legs and lungs had gotten stronger, she knew, and so had the shattered pieces of her soul. She zippered shut her shoulder bag, closed her eyes, and took a breath. Opening her eyes, she scanned the little apartment, making sure nothing tell-tale would be left behind. When the red door closed behind her, she double-bolted the lock.

She didn't plan on coming back.

Tail and Trail

They were watching the street, or a house, Jack figured. But which one? He downed the last of his black coffee, hoping he wouldn't have to wait too long for an answer.

Walk, Don't Run

Looping the adjustable strap of the black rubber bag over her head, Mona slid the bag against her hip and ribs and stepped out into the concrete-gray Seattle afternoon.

A little black umbrella sprang open in her hand as she went west on James Street.

"Look," Alex said intently. A woman had exited one of the houses. She was dressed in black, and wore black jogging shoes. Jack caught a glimpse of her face before the umbrella came up, as she turned left and went up the street.

Jack sensed the other vehicles keying their engines and he did the same.

The woman kept her umbrella low over her head, and held it at an angle so that it was hard to see her face. Walking quickly, she headed west toward the waterfront.

The sedan waited, let her go a short distance before following her, with the minivan behind.

Jack fell in line, well back, but able to keep the others in view. Alex did her best to copy down license numbers.

Mona noticed there were only a few people out on the streets, mothers and nannies picking up schoolchildren, older kids with bookbags on their backs. An occasional deliveryman. None of them was Chinese. Or Asian.

She opened her mouth slightly and sucked in air between her teeth as she went.

Her heart pounded a beat inside her ears.

It was a slow-motion pursuit, as if the stalkers were biding their time, waiting for the right opportunity. He wondered who was in the minivan. Paper Fan? More goons? How many men would it take to kidnap a woman? He brushed back the edge of his jacket, felt the reassuring grip of the Colt.

The odd procession rolled along.

The woman occasionally glanced behind her, but the rain had chased people off the streets. After several blocks, Jack wondered if she could maintain the pace, but she seemed to have the legs for it, never letting up.

The buildings got taller when she approached Pioneer Square, a tourist destination even in the rain. Scattered groups of tourists in wet plastic ponchos were taking flash pictures.

She zigzagged through Pioneer Square as if she knew where she was going, heading toward the railroad tracks, the bus terminals, the piers along the waterfront.

The sedan barged through traffic to keep up as she forged ahead, dodging the clots of tourist umbrellas, veering left as she left the square. Just beyond where the avenues ended, a set of block-long industrial buildings provided a truck thoroughfare that cut diagonally toward the terminals.

She'd walked that stretch before, and only occasionally seen deliverymen in vans and trucks. A convenient shortcut. Seeing no one around, she seemed to relax her pace. The gray minivan struggled to stay behind the sedan.

Abruptly, she cut left behind a series of warehouses lining a deserted road that ran parallel to the railroad yards. The truck route was desolate under the Sunday rain. No people around, perfect. She quickened her pace again.

The sedan turned sharply into the shortcut, speeding up toward the warehouse road.

Jack lost sight of them momentarily but found himself getting too close to the gray minivan. He was forced to slow down in order not to expose himself and then had to go around traffic at a red light.

When he saw them again, the sedan had slowed near an access ramp to the piers, and the minivan suddenly cut in front of it, disappearing into the truck road. The angle at which the sedan had stopped effectively blocked off the turn toward the warehouses.

Jack pulled over, wondering if they'd spotted his tail. He got out of the car and crossed the street, where he could see down the long road. Alex followed cautiously, eyeing the sedan.

"Stay back!" Jack snapped at her, drawing his Colt revolver. She ducked behind a metal Dumpster as Jack spotted the minivan moving past the warehouses, a long block away.

Hearing the squeal of tires behind her, Mona turned and saw the minivan screeching to a stop partway down the road. Two men jumped out of it and started sprinting toward her.

She froze for a second before tossing the umbrella and breaking into a dash toward the bay.

Jack saw the two men chasing the woman. Neither he nor Alex noticed the big man who appeared from between parked cars. The man had seemingly come out of nowhere, knife in hand. He was already jumping at Jack, who'd looked back instinctively over his shoulder. Reflexively ducking away, Jack twisted and brought his gun hand up, pointed toward heaven, and pulled the trigger. He heard Alex's scream mixed with the repeating thunder from the Colt, then two more explosions as the impact of the man's body bowled him over, slamming them both to the concrete pavement.

Jack squeezed off two more shots, the noise muffled against the heavyweight's body.

Almost there, Mona panted, just another block. The terminal loomed up ahead. She breathed in gasps but her legs were strong from the long jogs back to Chinatown.

Her lead lasted almost fifty yards.

The two men caught her and started pulling and pushing her toward the minivan, which had backed up onto the end pier. They pinned her arms and dragged her along, screaming and kicking. She tried digging in her heels but her sneakers skidded across the wet planking of the boardwalk. The abductors were carrying her toward the end of the pier. One of the men slapped her but she kept screaming.

Fuck! Jack felt blood oozing from his ear, adding to the shock wave washing over him, the man's bulk now a dead weight on top of him. It took two *shaolin* breaths before he could shove the man off.

The concrete pavement had banged a gong into his head, but Jack recognized the man as the goon with the nunchakus from the temple. His knife had skidded to a stop near the Dumpster where Alex crouched.

They continued forcing Mona along.

A small boat was moored illegally at the end of the pier. An older man stepped out of the minivan, angry at her screaming, and at the sound of gunfire. He barked some slang Cantonese at the two men.

"*Mo lun yung!* Both of you are useless! Go back and stall them!" He grabbed Mona by the wrist as the men scampered back toward the street. She twisted and resisted but was unable to break his iron grip. She was ready to scream again when he dug a fist into her belly that drove the air out of her, dropping her to her knees. He held her contemptuously by her hair as she gasped for breath.

There were police lights coming along the waterfront now; it seemed like forever before she got up on one knee. She was surprised at how strong the old man was as he started dragging her by the hair toward the waiting boat.

Jack twisted up onto his elbows, catching his breath. Apparently, they'd made him, and the big goon had slipped out of the sedan and doubled back. Ahead of him now, a second man exited the sedan and was coming in Jack's direction. The *shuriken*-throwing man. This time he had a gun in his hand.

"They're getting away!" Alex screamed, pointing toward the end of the pier where a man was dragging the woman along by her hair. Her screams had died out.

Jack pointed the Colt at the man, but it was empty. Ripping out his speedloader clip from his jacket pocket, he popped the Colt's cylinder clear of spent shells. He was on his knees now, trying to insert fresh rounds as the *shuriken* man closed in, taking aim and crouching.

The old man yelled something to the boatman and Mona heard the growl of an inboard motor revving up. Yanking her forward, the old man cursed and made ready to shove her onto the boat.

Her struggles had worked open the zipper of her shoulder bag. Suddenly, he pounded a heavy fist at her jaw, bloodying her mouth. She reeled backward and twisted down, reaching into the open bag. He continued chop-punching her in the back of the head. She thought she heard the wail of sirens.

The old man paused, looking back up the pier where he had dispatched the two 49s. The police lights were getting closer. He cursed again and turned back to Mona, cocking his fist to hammer her again.

The *shuriken* man smiled, sensing the kill. Suddenly, Alex stepped out from behind the Dumpster and picked up the dead man's knife.

"Hey!" she yelled.

Surprised to see her, he hesitated for a moment before aiming his gun her way. Alex reared back and flung the knife with all her might. The knife spun wildly through the air and the man ducked it easily, laughing, then cursing, *Dew!* He sneered and pointed the gun again, taking a step in her direction even as Jack felt the fresh bullets sliding into the Colt's cylinder, and snapped it shut.

The man glanced at Jack, who was braced on one knee now, leveling his gun and cocking the hammer. The fire exploding from the Colt's barrel froze the man until the first two .38 hollow points tore into his chest. The revolver roared rapidly again and the man dropped to his knees, glaring at Alex until the light left his eyes. He collapsed in a heap, the sneer gone from his face.

Jack ran over and kicked the gun out of his hand as the last gasp shuddered out of his body.

Alex ran toward the pier, and Jack ran after her, clipping his detective's shield to his jacket.

The new round of gunshots had distracted the old man.

Mona brought her hand out of the shoulder bag with the Chinatown souvenir letter opener in her grasp.

The last thing the old man saw clearly as he turned was the flash of something metallic in her hand, a spike, he thought, as she plunged it into his eye. His snarl froze on his mouth. The sudden pain shocked him. Blood streamed down his face. He staggered forward, his brain short-circuiting, *chi seen,* howling as he yanked the dagger from his eye.

There were police cruisers wheeling in, and a fierce commotion near the end of the pier. The two goons from the minivan waited by the access road, ready to block the way.

"Alex!" Jack yelled, knowing this time he had two shots left in the Colt. She froze as a tall white man in plainclothes suddenly ran up yelling, "Police! SPD!" then lowering the gun in his hand when he saw Jack's badge.

"NYPD!" Jack yelled back as they sprinted together toward the pier, a barking, panting exchange running between them.

"Detective Yu, I presume!"

"Right! You're Detective Nicoll?" Jack noted the man's chiseled features, the trim mustache.

"From a red ball to a tong war, brother!" Nicoll said, grinning.

Alex trailed behind them as they ran.

His grip never loosened even through the extreme agony and her fierce screams that filled his ears. She felt a searing pain from her wrist, as if the red bangle were on fire, burning her. She mustered what strength she had left and violently ripped herself free from him. She hardly noticed that something had loosened through the air, that part of his sleeve had gone limp. She bolted in a near-panic toward the water, stopping dead, gasping, when she came to the ten-foot plunge at the edge of the pier.

The old man willed himself onward, stumbling into the grasp of the thug in the boat. The thug then leapt onto the pier, going for Mona. She was already backed up to the edge, breathless, trying to shake off her dizziness from the blows that had pounded her head.

Flashing lights rolled across the boardwalk entrance. People, and running uniforms, yelling things in English.

The thug took several steps in her direction.

Save me, *kwoon yum*, Goddess of Mercy! She took three deep breaths before stepping off the pier, letting herself fall.

At the access road, a squad of SPD uniforms had bagged the two Chinese from the minivan. There was no one in sight down the long length of the pier. When Jack and Alex got to the end, there was only the sound of waves and the distant churning of motor boats across the bay.

"Gone," Alex said in disbelief. "All gone."

"A woman went into the water," Jack informed Nicoll. "And maybe a man, as well." They stared into the dark water beneath the pier as Alex gave Jack a napkin to sop up the blood clogging his ear.

"Harbor Patrol will pick up anyone in the water," Nicoll offered.

"Was a boat here?" Jack asked aloud.

"Coast Guard can check that out, too," advised Nicoll.

The three of them scanned the surface of the bay, looking for a body, clothing, *something*. All they saw were a couple of dead birds and the usual debris, shards of driftwood, a plastic soda jug.

The Seattle cops were out in force now, cordoning off the place where Jack had left two men dead.

"Did she witness any of that?" Nicoll nodded toward Alex.

"Unfortunately," Jack answered hesitantly.

"We'll need a statement from her," indicated Nicoll. He escorted Alex back along the pier toward the uniforms securing the scene.

Looking south down the waterways, Jack saw Harbor Island, and Duwamish beyond that. Northward lay an endless waterfront of piers, green parks, and commercial landings. Directly before him was the wide expanse of Elliott Bay, with freighters and ferries and assorted pleasure craft plying the frigid waters in every direction.

But no woman, and no man. No Paper Fan.

Jack checked the edges of the pier and saw a small dark stain on the wet planking. Upon closer inspection he saw it was dark red: a smear of blood. He stepped carefully, seeing several more tiny droplets that led to a pair of bollards.

Beside the bollards he saw what appeared to be a human hand attached to some kind of elastic strap. A man's hand, he thought, smeared with blood. The fingers were clenched around something red. Jack could see a curved fragment of a red bangle caught in its grasp. Examining the broken piece, he wondered if the unusual color was the result of its being covered in blood. In the rain, it felt slick. The bangle had broken clean through but the blood-red color held fast when he rubbed it.

He took out his plastic camera and snapped a few shots of the hand and the broken bangle. The hand felt heavier than he thought a prosthetic hand should, and he wondered if there were metal joints within.

He put it back near the bollard before advising the crime scene techs to bag it.

When he got to the turnoff, he saw that one of the SPD uniforms had found the knife more than twenty yards from where Alex had flung it. It had bounced and skidded along the concrete until it stopped beside the driver's door of a parked car. It was a *tantō*-style Japanese blade but with a serrated edge.

Watching them bag it as evidence, Jack felt chills thinking that the eight-inch razor-sharp blade was meant for his neck.

Alex leaned on the Dumpster with her fist against her chin, looking toward the bay. It had taken her a half hour to tell, and retell, her story. Jack could see the fatigue in her eyes, could hear the drag in her voice when she said, "I'm sorry, Jack. I've got to get back to the hotel, to catch an evening flight back."

"Can I get one of the uniforms to drive you?" Jack asked.

"No, it's all right," she declined. "I've got to return the car anyway."

"Sorry for the craziness," he said, giving her a big hug. She responded with a gentle kiss to his cheek, and he felt awkward, knowing she had to have the missing woman on her mind.

"Call me when you get back," she said.

"Sure," he answered.

"Promise," she insisted, knowing his police work always came first.

"Okay, *promise*," he repeated, watching her go as Nicoll took possession of the bags of evidence.

"These two are done," Nicoll said as CSU finished photographing the bodies.

Jack recounted events to Detective Nicoll, explaining how he'd tailed the men in the two vehicles, and how they tried to stop him from getting to the woman.

Dead on the wet concrete pavement was the big nunchaku-wielding man, with wounds to the upper chest and shoulder, and two closely spaced gut shots, courtesy of Jack, for trying to stab him in the back. He had a driver's license in his pocket that identified him as Shi Man Chun, from San Francisco. Jack could still feel the welts on his shoulder.

The other dead man was the big guy's partner, who'd

fancied himself a ninja assassin. Jack had drilled two hollow points into his chest that ripped out his back and shredded his rain jacket. One shot had missed, but the last one tore through his eye and blew out the back of his head. A puddle of blood was spreading in the rain.

He definitely wasn't assassinating anyone anymore.

Fuck him, Jack thought. He tried to kill me but I beat him to the punch. Deal. Next.

In his pockets they found keys, a small sum of cash, and an international telephone calling card. There was a New York driver's license that identified him as Tsai Ming Hui, rubber-banded together with several business cards. One of the cards was from a Hong Kong law firm, Wo Sun Partners, with a Tsim Sha Tsui address. Another card represented a New York firm, Chi and Chong, Esq., located on East Broadway. The last card was from a Mong Kok Jewelers Association. What surprised Jack was the name scrawled across the back of the New York lawyer's card: SHELDON LITTMAN. Next to it was the Chinese word TONG. It made clear who was paying Shelly high legal fees.

The techs bagged the bodies for the morgue wagon as Nicoll interrupted Jack's discovery.

"Congratulations, by the way," he said. "I heard you got your shorty, Eddie Ng."

"Patrol did a great job," Jack answered evenly.

"So you did good up here, Jack." Nicoll smiled under his mustache. "Killing two bad guys, taking a cold-blooded murderer home. Not bad for a few days in Seattle, huh?"

"Yeah," Jack agreed reluctantly, flashing back on the dead men's faces.

"And if anything new develops here, I'll update you."

"Thanks." Jack forced a smile. "I'd appreciate that." He felt the shock of the day slowly seeping into him.

"If there's a woman, we'll find her. And if anyone calls looking for a fake hand . . ."

Jack nodded, watching them load the body bags. Nicoll got into his unmarked car and followed the meat wagon to pick up the paperwork. Out by the access ramp the cops were hauling away the two remaining goons, and the terminal was quiet again.

Jack went back to the end of the pier and stood there looking out over the water for any signs from the Harbor Patrol or the Coast Guard. The harbor cops had responded to a boating accident off West Seattle, and Jack finally spotted them coming around the point. The Coast Guard had come through Puget Sound, a twenty-five-minute trip. Neither service had reported any sightings over the police band.

Jack waited on the pier until the last of the light, still hoping something would float up. In his mind, he reviewed the two times that he'd seen the missing woman, Mona. Once on a San Francisco rooftop, and now, on a Seattle pier. Based on the running glimpses he'd had, he couldn't say for certain that it was the same woman. Same general height and weight, sure, but between the short hair and the long hair, the sunglasses, and makeup or lack of it, he couldn't swear to it.

She'd eluded him again. Floating not only in the wind this time, but out to sea as well. He thought of the broken jade bangle in the prosthetic hand's grasp. How did it figure? Sooner or later, he knew, Mona was going to surface again.

He returned to his motel room, so exhausted that he didn't need the little vodka bottles from the minibar to help him crash.

On the Waterfront

Daylight found Jack back at the pier, watching the rain dapple the dark surface of the bay. The terminal area was busy with delivery trucks, tour buses queuing up, ferries docking, and smaller craft making ready to cast off.

He imagined the smell of coffee and croissants flavoring the salt sea air.

They never saw a body surface.

A Coast Guard cutter sliced across the rippling water, its wake white and choppy. Several times, Jack saw things floating: a waterlogged piece of luggage, an oil drum cloaked with barnacles and seaweed, a dead seagull drifting on a black garbage bag.

Nothing.

The icy water beneath the pier was maybe twenty feet deep, he thought, plenty deep enough to drown in, especially if someone was unconscious, or in shock, when they fell in.

Still, the divers hadn't found anything.

He was there an hour before Nicoll approached him, a cardboard cup of Seattle joe in his hand.

"I tried calling your cell," Nicoll said.

"My battery died," Jack explained.

"You *know* Harbor Patrol's on top of it, right?" Nicoll asked pointedly, firing up a cigarette.

"I know that."

"And you know your being out here won't make anything float up faster, yes?"

"I know that, too." The Coast Guard was checking flow charts, analyzing the currents, tides, the drag of big ships. The harbor cops had advised him that the riptides were fast, strong, and deep, twenty-five feet in some spots. The tides could suck a body down, swirl it around for days before giving it up. Bodies had been known to float up way south or north along coastal Seattle, and as far out as Alki Point.

Still, Jack felt the same way as he had that night beside Lucky's bedside, that somehow his presence at the scene might spark an idea, a memory, provide some clarity. He remembered that Ah Por's clues had been *yuh*, rain, and *seui*, water. *Water over water*, she'd concluded. Now he saw the connections: The attack had occurred in the rain, in a city known for rain. Mona had disappeared, possibly into the water, and *water over water* could mean the riptides.

He made a mental note to visit Ah Por when he got back to New York.

"So here's the update on the tong war," Nicoll announced with a grin. "The two we arrested were illegals. We're transferring them to INS for deportation. The two dead *hatchetmen*"—he finished his cigarette and flicked it into the bay—"came up from San Francisco. Motor Vehicles is still checking on the car and the minivan. And the license numbers your pretty lady friend copied down. The big man has a long sheet from Oakland, for gambling, and bootleg cigarettes. The Jap knife's got his prints on it. The other kung-fu fighter, was a little different. He freelances, somehow, for law firms, and he has a New York driver's ID. That's your neck of the woods, isn't it?"

"I think he's a player, but I'm not sure in what game yet," Jack added. How was he going to explain to ADA Bang Sing?

"A boat turned up abandoned near Harbor Island," Nicoll continued. "There were a few drops of blood and a Vicodin pill on it but nothing else. We'll see if there's a blood match with the hand, and we're canvassing the island for any witnesses."

"They were triads, dodging a Red Notice," Jack offered. "You'll get a call from INTERPOL."

"Yeah, okay. Plus we got this prosthetic hand. Bionic, real neat. Fingernails, knuckles, and creases even. Last made by a British company ten to fifteen years ago."

"And a piece of red jade," Jack added quietly. "Part of a broken bangle."

"What is that? Some kind of voodoo?"

"It's a Chinese thing," Jack said. "I'm not sure you'd understand."

"Well then, don't worry about it, Jack." Nicoll smiled. "Remember . . ."

"I know, I know," Jack responded wearily. "It's *Chinatown*."

Nicoll laughed, and Jack walked him back to his car.

"Look," Jack apologized, "I know I dumped on you during a red ball, but—"

"Hey, Yu, you came to *my* turf," Nicoll interrupted. "Dropped two bodies on *my* desk, and I closed it the next day. That's kudos for me, so don't sweat it, okay?"

"Thanks," Jack answered, watching Nicoll get in his unmarked Ford and drive away.

He'd figured them wrong, Jack realized. The Seattle cops had expressed racism in their tone and content, but they had been up front with it, unlike in New York where they'd play you with a smile and a wink before stabbing you in the back. He'd never condone racism but knew in the end that actions spoke louder than words.

Nicoll was a cop's cop above all, and Jack respected him for that. At game time, it was diligent police work by the Patrol Division that had brought about Eddie's collar at Julio's Place. And the SPD's arrival at the terminal pier had definitely interrupted the abduction.

They were professionals, after all, working the job.

Jack felt grateful as a Harbor Patrol boat cruised by. He left the pier, walking south through the mist. Gradually, he found the place by the bus stop, the El Amigo, where he ordered up a six-pack of *cerveza* and assorted dishes, and thanked Carlos and Jorge for their assistance. He gave them his detective's card and offered help if they ever needed it.

They finished the Dos Equis before the fajitas and enchiladas.

Back at the Sea-Tac Courtyard, Jack fell asleep thinking about *cerveza frio* and the icy waters of Puget Sound.

Swept Away

The full moon hung above the harbor and calmed the currents of the winter night. The freezing waters of the bay had welcomed her, embracing her in its tides and icy backwash, swirling beneath the piers and past the submerged pilings.

She'd held her breath into the murky depth, shock surrendering to numbness even as she saw the dim light above at the surface. In the whirling commotion of jetsam and wreaths of kelp, she imagined sea nymphs and sirens with beckoning smiles.

The gripping currents pulled her toward a stretch of pilings as she began her ascent from the bottom's darkness. No *bot gwa*, no *fung shui*, no red jade of luck. She kicked furiously, reaching upward with desperate arm strokes, clawing toward the surface, toward *kwoon yum*, her lungs ready to burst. . . .

Dead Man Flying

Eddie was quiet the whole plane ride back from Sea-Tac to JFK. Except once when he used the toilet and once when he was allowed to stretch his legs, Eddie stayed cuffed at his waist, braced in the window seat in the back section of the plane, blocked in by Jack.

Here was a guy, Jack thought, who showed no remorse for what he'd done, a guy who was looking at long-term lockup, and yet thought somehow his life was going to be normal again.

Jack remembered Ah Por's clues taken off Eddie's juvenile poster. *Yuh*, she'd said, rain. And *lo mok*, which he'd thought meant Negro. Rain was a symbol of Seattle, as in Mona's case, but *lo mok* here meant the surname Mok, or Mak, the same in written Chinese. Willie Mak, *lo mok*, was one of the killers at the Wah Mee Massacre, Seattle's worst crime ever.

Ah Por had pointed him in the right direction, though, of course, Jack didn't realize it at the time. He'd focused on the red star and monkey tattoos.

They landed without incident.

Jack cabbed Eddie back to lower Manhattan, feeling oddly enough that both of them were *home*. Jack could feel Eddie scheming even as he was turned over at the Tombs for detention. By the time he'd get a public defender he'd be at Rikers, with the rest of the New York City bad boys.

Maybe he'd get Punitive Segregation, for his own good, which, ironically, was where Johnny Wong was being held.

By the time he'd completed the transfer of custody at the Tombs it was 9 PM, too late to find Ah Por. Snow flurries filled the air. Captain Marino wasn't at the Fifth and Jack already felt jet-lagged. He was hungry, and considered calling Alex like he'd promised, but it was very late for dinner and he thought better of dragging her out in the snow and cold.

He'd been gone a week and really wanted to get back to Sunset Park, eat some Shanghai dumplings, shower, and sleep in his own bed. He went down to East Broadway and caught a Chinese *see gay*. The driver whizzed him across the Brooklyn Bridge with the window down a crack. He watched the night colors playing across the river, the thousands of sparkling lights dancing between the snowflakes, and imagined everything calling to him.

Welcome home.

Legal Blows

Overnight flurries had left a sloppy inch of frozen snow on the ground, and Jack was glad to be wearing his Timberland boots and down jacket again. When he arrived at the 0-Five the captain was in a morning meeting. The door to his office was closed and the desk sarge groused, "It could be a while."

Jack decided to get some hot tea and see if Billy Bow or Ah Por was around. He peered into the steamy window of the Tofu King and didn't see Billy. Ah Por wasn't on line for free congee at the Senior Citizen's Center. He decided to give Alex a call.

She was busy preparing a case but they agreed to meet at the Golden Star later that night. Jack decided to visit Lucky at Downtown Hospital before coming back to see the captain.

In the captain's office, Shelly Littman placed his silver Halliburton briefcase down at the short edge of Captain Marino's desk. He leveled his blue shark eyes at ADA Bang Sing and announced, "I've had witnesses come forward lately who will swear that my client couldn't have been at the scene, but that's just more background. Now, it seems, Detective Yu has even less of a chance to make his case than before. If I have INTERPOL testify about the possible abduction of this woman, with *witnesses,* mind you, and the corroborating reports of Seattle PD, not to mention that

Detective Yu shot and killed my legal assistant who was investigating this same woman *suspect,* there'll be a ton of questions and a ton of doubt as to my client having been the lone shooter of Uncle Four."

Captain Marino shifted uneasily in his seat behind the big desk, and ADA Sing twisted his mouth into a frown.

"You don't have a case, Sing," Littman continued. "I'll tear your detective up on the stand. The jury will love it. Every conflicting statement that comes out of his mouth—and I don't even have to mention the mess with Internal Affairs—allegations of corrupt behavior, etcetera—every word puts him deeper into the crapper. So here's the deal: my client has already confessed to buying the gun and loading it. That's all, guilty of *stupidity.* He cops to illegal possession of a handgun for time served. He'll probably lose his chauffeur's license, maybe his car."

Littman smirked. *Time served.*

To the captain, it seemed like ADA Bang Sing flinched at the thought of being accused of wasting taxpayers' money on a bad case. A politician's awareness. Marino knew they'd have to advise Jack, and would need to temper the decision to fold against the good job he'd otherwise done in Seattle.

Lucky to Be Alive?

At Downtown Hospital, it was just another frigid and gloomy New York City morning, with the EMS techs bringing in the frostbitten or frozen-dead homeless and the elderly. New immigrants with ashen faces waited patiently in the ER.

Jack wore his badge and cut straight to the CCU curtained-off space that was Lucky's room. The darkness of the morning had tricked Jack, and he half-expected to see the overnight nurse.

The life-support machine pumped rhythmically in Lucky's space, background sound for the electronic *ping* of the electrodes measuring his heartbeats. His cheeks had hollowed, sunken. How many more weeks before he'd become skeletal? wondered Jack grimly. He doubted Lucky had had any kind of health insurance, so the On Yee, who sponsored the Ghosts, were probably paying for the machine. They must believe that Lucky knows something, Jack surmised, secrets valuable enough for them to keep him alive.

"How much longer can this go on?" he heard himself say. When would the On Yee determine that Lucky was no longer important?

The resident neurologist had warned Jack against great expectations. "Even if he comes to, he'll likely have some brain damage."

Would he have forgotten the Ghosts? Or their secrets and memories of their childhood in Chinatown? Jack remembered their younger days, dashing across the black-tarred rooftops to their hiding places, and their childish hopes. Jack wanted to tell Lucky that he'd caught the punk who'd put the .22 slug in his brain, and wished Lucky could have understood the stupidity of dying over some stolen watches.

Unsure of what he was hoping to get from the motionless body, Jack left Lucky and turned his thoughts back to the Fifth Precinct.

Good News, Bad News

The office was open and the captain motioned Jack in before he could rap on the door.

"Welcome back, Jack," Marino began. "I want you to know I've put you in for another commendation. The chief thinks you did a good job bringing Eddie Ng back, and the DA's office thinks it's a solid case." He paused for effect. "You can put in for those days at regular pay but the department won't pay for airfare, hotel, or anything else."

Jack responded with a smile and a knowing nod as the captain handed him a fax sheet.

"This came in from Seattle headquarters, from a Detective Nicoll."

The fax confirmed that the blood workup was a match, that the blood on the bionic hand matched the blood found on the abandoned boat near Harbor Island and also on the fragment of the broken jade bangle. The report also noted scorch marks across the palm and fingers where the red bangle was grasped.

Jack felt the urge to visit Ah Por.

"I need to see all that in a report," indicated the captain. "It moves the case forward, no?"

Jack nodded. "Yes sir, let's see what else comes up."

But no missing females had floated up. And no one had

claimed a missing hand. Could it be Paper Fan's? Or one of the other thugs?

"By the way," Marino advised, "ADA Sing's coming in."

It sounded vaguely like a warning.

* * *

A minute later there was a rap on the door frame and Bang Sing entered. Jack stood to one side of Marino's desk and exchanged nods with the assistant district attorney.

Sing, with his Chow Yun-Fat good looks, measured his words carefully.

"I got some bad news, and then *worse* news," he said. This seemed directed at Jack, who noticed Sing pausing to take a breath, like a candidate about to deliver his speech.

"Eddie Ng has retracted his confession," Sing said. "He's now claiming that you coerced him, by making promises and threats. He alleges that you told him you'd let him be the Seattle jailhouse bitch if he didn't go along with the confession. That you'd let skinheads fuck him in the ass. He said that you were harder on him because he was Chinese."

"*So* much bullshit," groused Jack. "And you buy that crap?"

"It's just a delaying tactic. All the evidence will hang him," Sing said confidently. "Once you testify about the murder weapon and the matching ballistics, and the stolen watches he was caught with, he's done. The vic's prints are on the watch bag."

"The scheming little bastard," cursed Jack.

"Yeah, he might get a few Chinese or Asians on the jury but that cuts both ways. We'll nail him good, anyway. You did a great job."

So why doesn't it feel that way? thought Jack. Barely placated, he hissed, "So what's the worse news?"

Sing took another breath, and avoided eye contact with Jack.

"The Johnny Wong deal. We're going to accept a plea." Sing glanced toward the captain. "Illegal possession of a weapon, and reckless endangerment."

"You shitting me?" asked Jack incredulously.

Marino shook his gray-haired head, frowning.

"What's he get for that?" challenged Jack.

"Time served."

Jack grimaced, trying to contain his exasperation.

"I can't put you on the stand, Jack," Sing said apologetically. "I'm sorry. But you'd kill your own case. Plus, and I don't know *how* Alexandra got involved in all this, but she's a witness here as well. And you killed Littman's assistant? Trying to prevent a kidnapping? Of a missing woman who might be pivotal to the case? Shelly will *kill* you on cross."

Jack felt his heart sink, angry to hear the names *Shelly* and *Alexandra* in the same conversation.

"It's not your fault, Jack," offered Sing. "It's just how it happened. Maybe it was destiny. This woman, she played you as good as she played Johnny the chump. Everything's tainted. We have to cut our losses."

He wondered again about how Bang Sing might be connected to Alex, and felt uncomfortable in the stuffy overheated room. The captain's phone rang and Jack left the office without another word, never looking back.

He was cutting his losses.

Pain and Suffering

He found Ah Por in the Senior Center, at a small card table with a group of other old women, gray wizened elders playing *sup som jeung,* thirteen-card Chinese poker.

Ah Por showed her hand and cackled victoriously.

Jack caught her eye, offered a slight bow and a small smile. He had the *shuriken* and the snapshot of the bionic hand ready, along with two folded five-dollar bills. In his pocket he cradled the curved fragment of the red jade bangle he'd extracted from the grasp of the fake hand.

Ah Por backed her chair to the wall and allowed another wrinkled old woman to take her place. She looked at Jack, seeing his father in the face of the son, a man now.

"Your father was a good man," she said. "He was honorable."

Sure, thought Jack, but that wasn't what he was hoping to hear.

"Your shoulder is hurt," she said, eyes brightening as he recalled the bruise from the nunchakus. Ah Por always seemed to know about his wounds. "Your heart is heavy," she added. "But you have brought justice to two evil men."

Did she mean the two he'd shot dead? wondered Jack. Or did she mean Short Eddie or Paper Fan? He palmed one of the folded fives into her gnarled hand, carefully handed her the *shuriken*. She handled it gingerly, and looked at it closely for a few seconds.

"Sharp," she observed, "but no longer deadly. It belongs to a Hip Ching."

Not surprised, Jack exchanged the photo of the hand for the throwing star, palmed her the other five, and leaned in closer. She rubbed her fingers over the snapshot, taking several deep breaths.

"So much pain," she whispered. "He has a dragon in his eye." Jack felt like taking notes but knew to continue paying attention.

"Who?" he asked.

"A black snake," she answered quickly, glad to be returning the photo.

He gave her the broken red bangle.

Ah Por ran her fingers over it, caressing it, then pressed the red jade piece between her palms, putting heat into the precious stone. She put her head down and closed her eyes.

"*Aaya,*" Jack heard her moan. "So much pain." Again, Jack thought, perhaps she was confused, repeating herself. He knew better, and let her proceed.

"So much suffering," Ah Por continued. "Merciful Buddha, forgiveness and love survives all." She paused to catch her breath. Jack quickly gave her another five.

"What happened to the owner?" he asked.

What appeared to be a wrinkled smile, or a grimace, crossed her face.

"She has gone," she answered, "to a *choy gee lo.*"

Choy gee lo? pondered Jack, Cantonese for "a rich man." Another of her seemingly unfathomable clues.

Ah Por looked off into the middle distance, held the jade against her heart.

"Chicken-blood jade," she murmured. "Especially lucky. Red jade represents courage and will, but…" She seemed bewildered.

"Did you find this on a *say see?*" she asked. On a dead person?

Jack hesitated before answering, "No."

"Lucky, then." Ah Por concluded. "Forgiveness, and mercy always," she said, "survives all." She looked toward the other old women, and Jack took back the broken bangle, knowing he'd been dismissed. He left her at the card table, smiling and wealthier, anticipating the rest of her winter day.

Pieces of Dreams

He spent the rest of the afternoon in Sunset Park napping off his jet lag. He lay in bed and listened to the rain pelt the rooftops, doing a tap dance on his window air conditioner. He occasionally heard a chorus of car horns from Eighth Avenue, or the sirens of cop cars and ambulances.

In the darkness behind the drawn shades, he had a series of disassociated dreams. The one he vaguely remembered was the one about Ah Por, pointing to a location on a map, like she was at the head of a class.

Jack couldn't see the map clearly but when recalling her clue, *choy gee lo*, a "rich man," he thought of how "rich man" sounded like "richman" sounded like Richmond.

As in Richmond, a Chinese suburb of Vancouver.

The connection stunned him. But fatigue betrayed him again, as his dream broke up into a thousand jagged pieces, chasing him back into unconsciousness.

Wait Until Dark

It was only dinnertime but the Golden Star was already half full, a mixed-bag clientele of Chinese, black, and Puerto Ricans driven in by the cold. They were mostly spread out along the oval bar, bopping and drinking under the dim blue light. Candy Dulfer's saxophone wailed out of the jukebox setup and most of the booths were empty, but Jack spotted Billy by the green-felt pool table in the back.

Billy was watching two Latinas shooting money ball, his apparently upbeat mood encouraged by shots of scotch and the display of cleavage leaning across the spread of colored balls.

Jack caught Billy's attention with bottles of beer, and they moved to the end of the bar where Jack could watch the front door. They traded palms and Billy started right in, grinning like a fool.

"Caught the motherfucker in a poolroom, ha?" He laughed. "What the fuck did I say? Street always runs to street, right?"

They clanged bottles and Billy chased hot scotch with cold beer.

"And the boy tried to run?" He shook his head. "Shit, if I was the OTB shooter I'd run, too!" He drained the beer, ordered another.

"Whoa," Jack advised. "Slow down, brother. Night's young."

Billy was deaf to the warning.

"You did good, brother! I knew you would." He went on, "Another medal on your chest, kid! What kinda badge you get next? *Platinum?*"

Jack grinned. "*Fuck* you, Billy."

They banged bottles again, laughing.

"You know I love you, right?" Billy deadpanned.

"Fuck you again, Billy Bow."

"I was right, though," Billy challenged, "about you having to go out there, doing it *yourself.* Right?"

"You were right," Jack admitted.

"Fuckin' A."

The smell of chicken wings and calamari wafted out of the kitchen. Jack checked his watch but Billy noticed Alex coming through the front door first.

"Hey, ain't that the lawyer chick you keep getting the *bok tong go* for? The one with the kid?"

"Not so loud, man," Jack shushed Billy.

"Sorry. I'm divorced. Lawyers make me nervous. But watch it, bro. Baggage." Billy brought his attention back to the ladies at the pool table.

"Check you later," Jack said, motioning Alex to one of the booths. She was wearing the red jacket again, the one he'd remembered in his dream.

They ordered drinks and food, and she lit up a cigarette.

"So, welcome back," she said as they clinked glass.

Jack felt it would be better for Alex to just forget the shooting incidents, and spared her the confusing elements of the hand and the charm and the abandoned boat.

"Nothing ever came up," he explained simply. "They haven't found any bodies. *Yet.*"

"So we don't know what happened to them?" she asked through the smoky exhale.

"Maybe we'll never know. Also, I never told you the woman was a possible murder suspect."

The revelation seemed to take some of the sympathy out of Alex. She shook her head, then shrugged her shoulders, knowing Jack would keep homicide details to himself.

"Okay then," she said, ready to move on. It seemed unlike her, but Jack figured being back in New York, with her full workload, had brought her back to reality. She sipped her Cosmopolitan and eyed Jack curiously.

He pictured her from his dream again, swaying to music. Alex seemed more pensive than usual and Jack wondered if he was the cause. They shared a steak and a side of calamari. Jack could hear Billy's laughter over the music from the jukebox.

"What's on your mind, lady?" he asked.

She narrowed her eyes at him and he felt her lawyer persona returning as she spoke over the rim of the glass.

"I'm six months into a divorce process," she began. "My divorce law colleagues have advised me not to get involved with anyone. No entanglements, no semblance of infidelity that could surface in court."

He allowed her to continue, the words *entanglement* and *infidelity* buzzing in his ears.

"Can I trust you?" she asked coolly.

"Me?" He took a swig of his beer.

"You're a cop involved in some controversial Chinatown cases. I'm in your case files. You helped me avoid a D-and-D, and people have seen us together in Seattle."

"I don't think there's a problem," he said casually.

"Not legally maybe, but ethically . . ." She slipped into his side of the booth, nudged him over.

"Look," he said smiling, "I don't think I'd want to be an *entanglement,* legal, ethical, or otherwise. It wouldn't be right."

"What's not right is the spousal jerk's got himself a girl-friend, living it up in Westchester. And *I'm* the one who's supposed to behave?" She snuffed her cigarette, put her hand on his chest like she was feeling for the heartbeats. "You wouldn't want to get *entangled* with me?" she teased. "I'm not misbehaving, am I?"

"Well, as long as you're not *disorderly,*" he replied.

She laughed and he saw an opportunity to ask her about what had been nagging him.

"As long as we're talking *legal,*" he said, "what do you think about ADA Bang Sing?"

Alex was surprised. "Where's *that* coming from?" she asked. "Did you guys butt heads or something?"

"No," Jack answered. "Not at all."

"He's on one of your cases?"

"That's right."

She eyed him suspiciously but said, "He's brilliant, but mercenary. He goes whichever way the wind blows."

"So he always has the wind at his back," Jack concluded.

"That's right. But you're both on the same side, no?"

"Well, yeah . . ." Jack retreated.

"So you're plying me for this information and it's strictly professional?"

"Right."

"And *not* because, let's just say, because you're jealous? Or something?"

"Jealous?" Jack repeated. "Me?" He remembered she'd asked him that in Seattle. "Why would I be jealous? Does he have something I want?"

Alex was quiet for a beat before answering, "Don't know. What do you want?"

"I want to know if I give love, I'm going to get love back," he answered. "Sounds hokey, I know."

"Sounds like *quid pro quo.*"

"It's not a game to me." He finished his beer. "You'll know if it's there. Or not."

"This is beginning to sound like a trial. Like we're in court."

"Forget it," he offered. "I was just curious."

"Okay." She let it go but he knew his concerns were still unanswered. There was a burst of raucous laughter and he could see that Billy was shooting pool with the Latinas now, and he felt happy for him.

The Golden Star was getting crowded and Jack paid the tab, offering to walk Alex home. They went out into the winter night and she linked her arm through his as they walked. She didn't seem concerned about entanglements anymore.

"Come up for some sambuca," she said. It came out soft but sounded like a command.

"You think?" he asked, still wondering about Bang Sing.

"Yeah, well, you have an outstanding rain check. You need to cash it in before something else happens," she insisted.

"Okay then," Jack agreed. "Good to go."